UNCHARTABLE:
ON
ENVIRONMENTAL
UNKNOWNS

2019 | VOL. 65

EXCEPTIONAL POETRY
AND PROSE SINCE 1956

Portland State University
Portland, OR

Portland Review 2019, Unchartable: On Envirnomental Unknowns

Copyright © 2019 Portland Review

Portland Review
Portland State University
P.O. Box 751
Portland, OR 97207 USA
http://portlandreview.org

Cover Art: Arabella Proffer, Manor House
Cover Design: Jessica Fonvergne & Kathleen Levitt
Interior Design: Jessica Fonvergne & Kathleen Levitt
Portland Review Logo Design: Rosie Struve

Printed in the United States of America

Portland Review is published by the graduate students in the English Department at Portland State University.

ISBN: 978-0-9974617-3-2

STAFF

LETTER FROM THE EDITORS

Greetings Readers,

Welcome to our 2019 themed anthology. This year, we wanted to collect stories, poems, essays, and artwork by authors with what John Keats called negative capability, a distinguisher that marks one as "capable of being in uncertainties, Mysteries, doubts, without any irritable reaching after fact and reason." The following collection features work by just such writers from all over the world.

Our goal this year was to find and publish art that grapples with the environment in the widest sense of the word. We uncovered explorations of impossible skyscrapers, the uncertainty of space, complex minds inside strange bodies, weather phenomena, insects of all sorts, dark forests, cathedrals, and hotels in Eastern Europe.

Each piece operates on its own, but we believe that, as a whole, the following collection exists as a small, delightfully inadequate field guide for charting out spaces of uncertainty.

Thank you to our contributors. Your writing inspired us, and made this collection come together in ways we never anticipated or expected. Thank you to our faculty advisors.

This book would not be half as aesthetically stunning without the patient and kind assistance of Professor Janice Lee. Thank you to all of the student editors who spent time making this anthology into the book you now hold in your hands. We couldn't have done it without you. Thank you to our readers. Your support and engagement means the world to all of us in here.

Jessica Fonvergne & Kathleen Levitt

Editors-in-Chief
2018-2019

TABLE OF CONTENTS

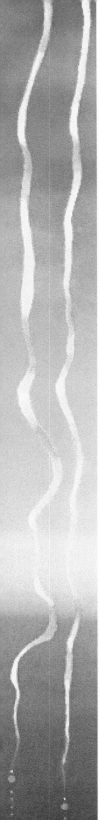

DAYS OF UNCERTAIN GREEN

Daryl Scroggins

Spring, and the discovery that my coat is three sizes too large. I know the different rooms of it. A cavern of wet wool in snow that turns to rain. For months, under my bridge, I raise my arm from water and drink at my own shoulder. My old home gone to doctors I can't see.

That time of pasting photos of myself on strangers. Wheat paste. Applied with a soft touch, but still—their shoulders warping away from danger. Gloved hands bowing my head below flashing lights, and then a jumble of people moving in cells. The sound of many pigeons under a trestle.

The watercolors a lady brought for me once, to lure me out, have wept from the edges of their tin case. I build nests for birds and wait, on into summer. A wasp examines one made of chopsticks and watermelon rind. A raccoon peers into a tangle of licorice and bright finishing nails. Then a mockingbird settles in a china cup set in a cat skeleton. I fight sleep.

A windy, no-thought day. I calculate my heart rate by barely touching my teeth to my teeth, tapping it out. The city deploys its vehicles in miniature vistas. A man comes with the mood of one checking on some report of me. A patch covering one eye; his other gazing as a whale would a moment before slipping below. He must see no cause.

I wonder how I can hold a day of colors, in rain, without bringing a bowl for the fire of it. The sea at this city's edge marks a kind of hollow, always seeming to say we should be amazed by any dry land. Out, and down among buildings, I slip into the damp echoes of the aquarium. Sharks rasp their gray skins against my sense of water, watching a vision of watchers. Outside, everything flies up with cries.

Going, arriving, going back. Leaving one place, I see myself gone from all of them. I wonder why some motions can't be canceled out, saving only the view until even that takes wing. So, bird, the blink of days, come to my eye beak first—swim into me. Find that avenue that falls through autumn to black bones, where perch the reasons.

PINK MOON

Silas Plum

HIGH RISE: A FINAL REPORT

Matt Leibel

Report #: 1-394-572XXXX
Building Address: [CONFIDENTIAL]
Inspector: [REDACTED]

Summary of Findings:

Inside the building is a small planet. The planet is named L'il Earth and is approximately three meters in circumference. It is inflatable and has a little clear plastic inflation nipple sticking out in the middle of the Atlantic, about 100 kilometers due west of the Azores. Back when people worked inside the building, they used to bat L'il Earth around during meetings, blissfully unaware that L'il Earth was a fully functioning planet with a fully functioning L'il Ecosystem, L'il Flora and Fauna, L'il Humans, L'il Infrastructure, etc.—all of which they were destroying, by treating it as a beach ball. These same workers may have been equally ignorant of the theory that our earth may in fact be the L'il Earth of some other much larger planet, and so on and so on—such that the infinite yet disposable nature of the universe is suggested Matryoshka-doll-like by this cheap toy globe that someone bored with the office décor once bought at a drug store for a buck ninety-five.

~

Inside the building is a vending machine. The machine dispenses edible replicas of other buildings. Among these are the world's most iconic structures: the Eiffel Tower, The Taj Mahal, The Statue of Liberty, The Sydney Opera House, the Kremlin, the Pyramids of Giza, etc. But instead of tasting like candy or chocolate, the buildings are artificially engineered to taste exactly as you would imagine those buildings tasting: building-flavored buildings. The vending machine is covered with decades of dust from disuse.

~

Inside the building is an artificial waterfall. Even the water itself is artificial, manufactured on the seventy-ninth floor out of synthetic hydrogen and oxygen molecules that are forced to awkwardly mingle, like co-workers at a bad office party. The artificial water tastes just like regular water, but it can kill you if you drink it.

~

Inside the building is an elevator. 681,426 people have used it. On the elevator, there have been 18,962 conversations about the weather. There have been 3,438 serious flirtations, and 1,567 cases of in-elevator harassment. The elevator has become stuck between floors 961 times. There are twenty-seven buttons on the elevator wall, including two emergency buttons and a fifteenth floor button that does not work, and has never worked. It is unclear what is on the fifteenth floor, or indeed if the fifteenth floor exists. There have been seventeen full-fledged sexual encounters in the elevator, five of which have involved more than two people. Four people have died on the elevator. Three marriage proposals have taken place, one of which was filmed, and received considerable attention in the local press. The other involved a lonely young man who proposed marriage to the elevator itself. The elevator has yet to give a response, though the man rode it up and down religiously every weekday, for five years of his life. The elevator remains eerily quiet, as if still weighing this offer.

~

Inside the building is a child's playground. The children who once played here have since grown up, lived their lives, and died—all within the playground's confines. Now there are only seesawing ghosts, tetherballing apparitions, spirits of the monkey bars: a haunting hinting at the very idea of children, a chilling personification of the high cost of lost time.

~

Inside the building is a library. The only books in the library are books about the building itself: the history of its design and construction, the chronicles of the people who have lived and worked within its walls, and the items found inside it. In fact, much of this report has been cribbed from the books within this library. The library is not a lending library, and this prohibition is strictly enforced: if even a single one of the books is removed without proper approval, the building will not only cease to exist, it will cease to ever have existed. Even the very idea of buildings itself may well be forgotten—reduced to bits of dirt too small to be recognizable as rubble.

~

The building contains the blood and sweat of all the people who were involved in constructing it so many decades ago. But it does not contain their tears: their tears are stored in a separate facility, where they are studied as part of a Top Secret government study on suicide rates among construction personnel. Later, the tears are desalinized, and evaporated back up into the clouds. Then the tears of the building's original builders rain down on us, reminding us of all the sacrifices that dot the landscapes we take so much for granted.

~

The ghosts of four of our former presidents are lurking somewhere inside the building. They sit around a ghost table, playing Hearts and telling one another their most embarrassing secrets and deepest regrets. The tidbits they casually toss out are the kind most historians would kill for, so it's critical, for the public's protection, that no historian ever be allowed inside, where 1000 hours of cassette recordings of secret presidential-ghost conversations await transcription.

~

Inside the building are many impossible things: clocks set to the wrong hour; a lost language spoken by a tribe that only exists theoretically in a book of speculative history; a copy of the Declaration of Independence from the Declaration of Independence, a little known manifesto from one of the earliest and most obscure anti-American separatist groups;

a lamp that generated all of its electricity from mice riding bicycles (until the mice died); a service elevator that only stops at prime-numbered floors; a regulation-sized Olympic swimming pool filled entirely with ketchup.

~

Inside the building are all the lies and false promises that have ever been told by humankind since the beginning of time. These have all been digitized and stored on a single server. Included among these lies and false promises are all the words to every book ever written—even (and especially) the ones that purport to tell the "truth" about our world. Among the lies archived in this database is the lie that this database, in fact, exists.

~

The building worries about whether it is up to code: not in a municipal sense, but in a moral one. Sometimes the building feels guilty for looking the other way at the myriad transgressions that have taken place, over the years, within its walls. But then it remembers: it has no control over any of this. In the end, it's just a fucking building.

~

Inside the building is a full-sized map of the opposite of the world. That is, only the places one can never get to are listed on the map: potential cities that never materialized, roads that continue past dead ends, lakes that dried up before the rain that formed them even hit the ground. It is the world's most comprehensive compendium of nonexistent places, and was intended to be marketed as an anti-travel guide for those who were, for whatever reason, philosophically against the idea of leaving home, loath to venture outside the safe confines of their adventurous imaginations.

~

Inside the building is a café featuring a coffee maker that dispenses every varietal of coffee on earth, including many varietals that have not yet been discovered. It is machine as Anthology of All Possible Coffees, a glimpse into the gaping yaw of the infinite. The café menu itself is also infinite, and printed in an infinity of languages, in tongues both possible and im—. And yet, it is also infinitesimally tiny, printed in the world's smallest font, and as such, the menu weighs less than a single coffee ground.

~

Inside the building is a fire extinguisher. Only instead of putting out actual fires, it has been designed to work only on metaphorical "fires": last minute emergency requests from clients, printer's mistakes on ready-to-be mailed pieces, co-workers losing their minds, etc. Once, there was an actual fire inside the building. Someone grabbed the metaphorical fire extinguisher and tried to put it out, to no avail. Eventually, the fire department did arrive, and the building was saved. But still, workers in the building wondered, what do fire fighters call it, down at the station, during the slow times, when they have internal metaphorical "fires" to put out?

~

Inside the building, there once was a photographic exhibition featuring stills of all the people who had, over the years, leapt from the building's high-floor windows to their deaths. Admission tickets were sold for substantial sums. The photos were accompanied by brief biographical sketches of the jumpers, along with speculations, often wild, as to what may have driven them to jump. As the show wound down, several of the photos were eventually auctioned off to the highest bidder—often without the permission of the subjects' families. Sometimes, sadly, family members would attend these auctions and bid on the photos of their loved ones, caught in the final act of their lives, in order to prevent such intimate moments from falling into the hands of well-heeled and conscienceless strangers. The legality of these auctions was never clarified—the enforceability of outside laws inside the building has always been subject to fierce debate.

~

Inside the building is a studio where, once, a beauty pageant was filmed. Only it wasn't a pageant involving bottle-bronzed silicone-enhanced women forced to tap dance in sashes while fielding broad queries about world peace, but a pageant in which linguistic feeling-state abstractions competed against each other, for scholarship money and pride. Contestants might have included Anxiousness, Benevolence, Calm, Pride, Anger, Love and Joy. One year, Poise had to be disqualified: it was both a contestant and a criterion upon which the contestants were judged. According to reports, no one who attended any of these feeling-pageants ever went home with the same conception of what beauty means that they had going in—which meant that the pageant had, indeed, done its job.

~

Inside the building is a building inspector. The first time the building inspector ever saw a high-rise, she had just come from a visit with her family to the zoo. So from a young age, she had deliberately conflated animals and buildings. She fancied the thought of buildings as particularly gigantic animals; sometimes frightening, like a T-Rex with monstrous teeth, sometimes calm and gawkily graceful, like a giraffe. Later on, in architecture school, her showpiece project ideas involved buildings inspired by the shapes of animals. She also sketched buildings as donuts, rollercoasters, mathematical equations, and giant slabs of Swiss cheese with holes in them. Very little of this dream thinking was either structurally sound or people centric, and the building inspector was forced to reassess her career plans. What she would come to realize, as an inspector, is that even buildings that look generically gray on the outside are endlessly bizarre when examined from within, as labyrinthine as the chambers of a heart. Each building is, she firmly believes, its own class of animal.

~

Things one could theoretically fill the building with, if you hollowed it out: gumballs, popcorn, pennies, snowflakes, smaller buildings, Gideon's Bibles from every Days Inn in the world, Terra Cotta Warriors produced by the first Han Chinese Emperor, early twentieth century pornography, prize pigs, robotic dogs, tricycles, tricorn hats, New Year's whistles, Jell-O, labyrinths, poker chips, chess pieces, snap judgements, snapping turtles, hollowness itself, the combined sounds of all lovemaking ever everywhere, St. Louis Style Beef Ribs from TGI Fridays, monkeys, cotton swabs, falsehoods, the letter Q, atrocities, air conditioners, conspiracy theories, literary theories, thesauruses, tigers.

~

Inside the building, one could sense the presence of God. Maybe this was because God used to drop by pretty often, working on the electrical wiring, repairing cracks in the walls, removing rusted nails, fixing gaps in the floorboards, listening to reggae music on an old boombox, and eating the tuna sandwiches God's wife had packed in a yellow metal lunchpail with the words "THE LORD" written in magic marker on a piece of masking tape. The day that God finally stopped showing up, it signaled the beginning of the end of the building: it had become a godforsaken space.

~

Sometimes, the building wishes it were a cloud. Sometimes the building wishes it were a bird, or a tree, or an airplane. Sometimes the building wishes it were a moon and a planet. Sometimes the building wishes it could jump over smaller buildings. Sometimes the building wonders whether buildings are built by people or people are built by buildings. Sometimes the building wishes it could lean over on its side, like that old tower in Pisa. Sometimes the building wishes it was Fort Knox, and a rousing heist scene were filmed within its walls. Sometimes the building wishes it could leap tall Supermen in a single bound. Sometimes the building wishes it could love, and be loved.

~

The building is untroubled by its own potential phallic connotations. If on some level, the original engineers built it quite so tall as a form of perhaps subconscious compensation for something…well, then that's on them. Buildings do not think of such things. Though it would be naïve of the building to assume that intimate liaisons didn't take place inside its walls, and quite frequently, too. In fact, the building, if pressed, could name the date, time and location of most, if not all, of these assignations.

~

The building as weapon: the building could be armed with gun turrets or shoulder-fired rockets. Archers could be positioned on the ninety-sixth floor. The building could fall over on top of smaller buildings, demolishing them. The building could serve as a lookout point for snipers or military strategists planning an invasion of a neighboring town. War games could be conducted within the building. Urban conflict could be simulated. If you shot bullets into the building's outer walls, would it bleed? Would it call out for a medic to wrap it up in a tourniquet before it headed back to the battlefield? Does the building mourn all the other buildings bombed in war or attacked with explosives by (problematic term here) terrorists? Does the building feel a burning desire for revenge?

~

The building, considered as a narrative. Buildings look like Capital Letters. Often this is an "I" but in some cases it's an "L," or as in the Gateway Arch, a lowercase "N." Rows of buildings can form words, or even sentences. A city of buildings tells a Story. Any building can be a library: full of books, music, papers, reference materials, containers of history and knowledge. The building knows more about us than we know about it. The knowledge that a building contains is often dangerous. Maybe this is why this building has been slated for upcoming demolition: it is the keeper of knowledge that is to be feared, and thus must be destroyed.

~

The slow build. Leap tall buildings in a single bound. If you build it, they will come. We built this city. More songs about buildings and food. Building blocks. Building bridges. Building to a climax. Elvis has left the building. Go ahead and build it out. It comes with a built-in bookshelf. We can rebuild it. Build a better mousetrap. Build your vocabulary. Build your self-esteem. Bildungsroman. Built for speed. Built to last. Built to order. Built Ford tough. Built in the good ol' US of A. Built like a brick shithouse.

~

Inside the building, the building inspector thinks of the young man in love with the elevator as she drafts her final report. She pictures him removing his shirt, to reveal a series of electric buttons lining his chest. She imagines that when he approaches the elevator, his buttons light up like bright ideas. She thinks of the elevator. To be desired like that: the polar opposite of objectification, an object perceived as a person. She has never experienced such earnest, displaced coveting. Confidentially: it intrigues her. She wonders what the young man will feel when he realizes the elevator's, and the building's, impending fate. Will he simply move on to another building? Will he, in his post–elevator–lust life, be able to push the same buttons of desire? Or will he perhaps move on to a new obsession: an Eames chair? A wall clock? A stress ball? A fire escape? A bonsai tree?

~

By the time you are reading this, the building will be gone. It will belong to the past: which is the only thing any of us can remember. And yet, the past is completely unreal: it is something we cannot touch. Unlike a brick, say, or a floorboard, or a breast. By the time you are reading this, the building will belong only to history. The contents of this report will lodge themselves in your mind as a mental structure—a brain building. For this inspector, the destruction of the building is unbearably sad. It makes the world less full, less interesting. It leaves a hole, as inconvenient and painful as a lost tooth. She might even posit that the building, though specifically constructed with metaphor-resistant materials, is a metaphorical stand–in for the world itself. The fact that you are reading this now suggests that the world has outlasted the building. But what kind of world can this be? Can it be one worth living in? How does one go on when one's quotidian reality has been snatched out from under her, like a magician-yanked tablecloth? Such questions obviously lie outside the scope and purview of this report.

BLISTER BOUNTY

Arabella Proffer

AT THE END OF AN EMPTY SKY

Sarah Janczak

A full rotation   to nightfall
takes hours,
        which is months

to a sleeping dog,   years
for the wasps.
       Their unrelenting nest
hovers over   my front door.
I did not invite them here.

A can of poison   sits on a shelf
in the mostly empty
       two car garage.

Small geckos in that same corner,
live above the door.
       The stray cat,

whose home is in the sewer   hides
in the rosemary.
       Honestly,
I would rather have
       a dozen stings forever on my back

than live without this
daytime moon   we can watch

turn translucent
       to effervescent

without ever   feeling
feet move   at all.

A QUIET DAY
WITH THE WEST ON FIRE

Margot Kahn

Upstairs, a boy hums while he plays. Inside a Mason jar, a caterpillar rests on the branch of a plum tree. Cake sits on the counter. Bread cools. A tomato ripens even as we hold our collective breath waiting for the wind and rain. We've asked ourselves a thousand times: *Why are the things we need the most the same things we take most for granted?* I watch the caterpillar sleep. I listen to the boy sing. Do they know how breathlessly I love them? In these days of smoke and haze, I hold onto the smallest things. My fear is as suffocating as any particulate matter, my heart as boundless as the sky we used to know.

THE INSTRUCTIONS

Marvin Bell

Sometimes late at night the voice from the radio begins to
      buzz from shifts in the atmosphere.
The voice repeats itself, no matter what it is saying.
I try to hear it as if it is addressed to me, but I can't make it
      out.
I hear something ominous in its unintelligibility, as if an
      approaching tornado was distorting the alarm.
The voice sounds knowing, secure in some underground
      bunker.
It is telling me what to do, and to do it now.
By morning, the voice has dematerialized, lost in space.
I stay in my room like a dog in a doghouse surrounded by
      noise.

PULSE

Marvin Bell

Glass is part of the story, and blood.
Metal filings and wood shavings are likewise a portion.
The cloth that covered table radio speakers shimmies.
In the story, where flies glisten and worms throb.
There in the story is the beating of a pulse.
That cannot be restrained, everyone can see it.
He is certain they can tell by his wrists.
By the bend in his embarrassed walk.
The new way of skipping a beat without seeming to move.
He tries to squeeze it away at the thumb.
The rapid delineations of his body perplex him.
It is the same with countries, but that's for later.

OREGON FEVER

Camellia Freeman

The stories Americans have wanted to tell about Oregon are the stories they have most wanted to believe about themselves, and about America itself.
—*from* Landscapes of Promise: The Oregon Story 1800–1940

In 1843, during the early stages of *the Fever*, a man by the name of Peter H. Burnett organized the first major wagon train from Independence, Missouri to Oregon's Willamette Valley. According to Burnett, Oregon's *fertile soil, extensive valleys, magnificent forest, and mild climate meant that it was admirably fitted for a civilized and dense population . . . for a cultivated race of men.* He lived in a world in which one's habitation determined one's future. If the right people were wed to the right land, both would benefit, together fulfilling some glorious destiny.

After arriving with nearly 900 emigrants in the Promised Land, Burnett took up his cause with a sort of furious vision by assisting in the development of the Provisional Government of Oregon and joining Oregon Country's Legislative Committee. The judicial system of this provisional government was led by a single supreme judge, and, in 1845, Burnett was the first supreme judge to be elected by the legislature. Regarding Burnett's early years, a fellow emigrant wrote that *no other single individual exerted as large an influence in swelling the number of home-building emigrants in Oregon.*

At the age of nineteen, Burnet changed his surname to Burnett with two ts for it was more *complete and emphatic* that way. Even as a young man, he'd recognized that if you wanted something, you had to take it. Paradise doesn't exist until you make it your own. *Besides*, Burnett added in defense of emigrant settlements, *the land appeared to be theirs for the taking; the natives had almost entirely disappeared from the lower section of*

Oregon. Only a small and diseased remnant was left. To Burnett, it was simply uncharted wilderness.

~

For most of Oregon's recorded history, many indigenous tribes and the majority of its non-indigenous population have resided in the Willamette Valley, one of the most fertile regions in North America due to its rich deposits of glacial till from over 12,000 years ago. One letter boasts: *Perhaps there is no country in the world that offers more inducements to enterprise and industry than Oregon.* It describes wheat *larger than any I have seen*, potatoes *abundant*, and growing *less than a mile from this place, a turnip* that will *likely exceed five feet* in circumference by harvest.

Approximately seventy percent of Oregonians inhabit the valley today, which extends 150 miles along the Willamette River as it runs north toward the Columbia. To the east are the sharpened Cascades and on its west the dense hills of the coastal range. Drive an hour or so west and you'll come upon the Pacific with its 362 miles of public shoreline, often described as rugged, secluded, unspoiled.

I grew up in this Promised Land. I was born in Good Samaritan Hospital high on a hill in the city of Corvallis— Latin for *heart of the valley*—as was my father and my daughter. Even my mother, who emigrated from Seoul in her mid-twenties, calls herself half-Oregonian, having now spent more of her life in Oregon than in Korea.

Just over a century after Burnett's arrival, my father's parents moved from Seattle to Corvallis in 1946. For the next thirty-five years, my grandfather worked for the *Corvallis Gazette-Times* as a reporter and editor. My grandmother advocated for local parks, worked as a middle school librarian, belonged to the Garden Club, the Friendly Club, and played bridge and golf. They built their modest home on a pretty half-acre, raised three children whom they dutifully taught about their Norwegian, German, and English ancestry, and are now buried in a cemetery that boasts views of the Cascades.

Perhaps they—and this non-Korean, white lineage in myself I am tracing—are something like what Burnett had in mind when he wrote *cultivated and civilized*—qualities that he believed made one deserving of the land and vice versa. In 1947, *Life* magazine referred to this region during post-war America as *a land of promises come true*.

~

During the five years he spent in Oregon, Burnett settled in a part of the Willamette Valley northwest of what is now Portland. He had grown up in Tennessee and lived in Missouri before pioneering west. Ever onward and upward, by 1848, he'd exchanged his faith in Oregon with faith in gold and joined the rush to California. One year later, he became California's first elected governor.

Despite men like Burnett moving on, the Fever continued *raging like any other contagion*. A letter from Iowa Territory signed *H* explains. Of someone who has caught the Fever, H writes: *With him there is always a land of promise further west, where the climate is milder, the soil more fertile, better timber and finer prairies. And on, on, on, he goes, always seeking and never attaining the Pisgah summit of his hopes.* To catch the Fever was to believe that Oregon, of all the unique wildernesses on the known continent, promised the greatest potential for achieving some utopic, God-ordained existence well worth risks of injury, disease, and even death. It was to believe beyond reason.

The Fever gained momentum from the 1840s to the 1860s, coinciding with the region's metamorphosis from British-American disputed Oregon Country to the United States' Oregon Territory in the latter 1840s to Oregon, the thirty-third state in 1859. An estimated 400,000 to 500,000 people traveled the rutted trail that began in Missouri, ran through Kansas, Nebraska, Wyoming, Idaho, and finally arched from one side of Oregon to the other like a rainbow.

As late as 1882, the *Corvallis Gazette*—the same newspaper my grandfather would build his career upon—reported this pronouncement on an immigrant wagon passing through La Grande: *In God we trusted / In Nebraska we busted / And now we are bound for the promised land.* Even fifty years after the earliest wagon trains, the familiar promise of Oregon as a second chance at Eden—where the earth can yield all you hope for, where it can be *yours*, where you can escape the problems that plague the Midwest and live as you please, nestled in a tidy cut of paradise—this promise, this Fever, abounded. It is what united the people who founded this state, wrote the laws, distributed federal land, and ultimately determined its fate.

~

Burnett—himself once a slave owner—wrote the bill that declared slavery illegal in 1844. But Burnett's bill had nothing to do with the ethical ramifications of slavery and everything to do with being anti-black. He intended *to keep clear of that most troublesome class of population* by discouraging free black persons from settling in the region. *We are in a new world*, he wrote, *under most favorable circumstances, and we wish to avoid most of the evils that have so much afflicted the United States*. According to the bill, all slaves were to be removed within three years, and any free black adults needed to remove themselves from the territory after two years for men and three for women. Originally, ignoring this legislation would result in *not less than twenty nor more than thirty-nine stripes*, a punishment later repealed, but only in exchange for the amendment that violators would be hired at *public auction, with the employer responsible for removing the black person when his service was ended.*

In his autobiography, Burnett responded to accusations of cruelty regarding these laws by explaining that he knew they would not necessarily be enforced—he claimed that the above *Lash Law* was not—but were written to *aid in founding a state superior in several respects to those east of the Rocky Mountains*. He *therefore labored to avoid the evils [. . .] of mixed races*. Burnett's vision of a superior state, his Promised Land, was a 200 million-acre home for whites only. A place uncontaminated by the *disenfranchised and troublesome class*.

~

Unlike much of the known world, it is not difficult to imagine Oregon two and a half centuries ago, before I-5 and the big box stores and microbreweries, before Nike and McMenamins and the Shakespeare Festival, before grass seed farms and cattle ranches, landfills and paper mills, dams and visitor centers and ranger stations, before the lumber roads and campgrounds, and even before the wagon ruts and bushwhacked trails and fur traders with beaver pelts one-two-ing their backs. Go past Meriwether Lewis and William Clark standing on the Columbia River Estuary, believing it to be the Pacific, declaring, *Ocian in view! O! the joy*. Back to a time when indigenous peoples lived without western industry and laws did not come from an empire and borders were fluid. Oregon as the Western Fertile Crescent. Here come the arrow, the pictograph, herbal remedies, and hordes of caught fish flinching weakly like jewels dimming in the sun.

It is easy to imagine Oregon when it was beauty incarnate, pristine, free of waste and technology and excess. It is easy to imagine because it is the Oregon Story. One in which the single most distinct quality of this state is its un-contamination—also its most coveted feature.

~

The Promised Land begins as an idea but refers to an actual place. It has a particular soil and topography with borders both natural and negotiated. When you finally get there, the work of harnessing paradise, of apportioning the land and demanding it yield, has only just begun.

In 1841, Congress passed the Distribution-Preemption Act to encourage American settlement in Oregon Country, which included modern-day Oregon, Washington, Idaho, and parts of Montana and Wyoming. Settlers could claim up to 160 acres at $1.25 an acre.

Two years later in 1843, the year Burnett arrived in Oregon Country, Willamette Valley residents drafted a constitution and—without signing treaties with the indigenous tribes—decided that settlers could claim up to 640 acres of land for nothing.

Each time the region's government changed hands, settlers needed to arrive at a new agreement. The most significant distribution of land came in 1850 during the era of American-run Oregon Territory. The Oregon Donation Land Claim Act granted 320 acres of federal land to white male citizens who already resided on that property (a married couple could get 640 acres) and 160 acres to any white male resident (320 acres for couples) who might migrate in the future. *Half-breed Indians* were allowed to make such claims because of their white fathers; *free blacks* were not.

~

The American people of the Oregon Territory passed their first exclusion law prohibiting the residence of *Negroes or mulattoes* in 1848. This was the same year that Burnett left the valley for the prospect of California gold, but the fear he had helped cultivate remained, now simply part of the landscape. The law's preface explained that *it would be highly dangerous to allow free negroes or mulattoes to reside in the Territory, or to intermix with the Indians, instilling into their minds feelings of hostility against the white race.*

Though that first exclusion law was repealed in 1854, in the 1857 November election, when debates over slavery were erupting across the nation, voters answered two significant questions: 1.) *Do you vote for slavery in Oregon?* 2.) *Do you vote for free Negroes in Oregon?*

Over seventy-four percent voted against slavery, and eighty-nine percent voted against *free Negroes*. Thus, a new exclusion law was born in which *free Negroes or mulattoes* could not *reside or be within this state, or hold any real estate, or make any contracts, or make any suit therein*. Anyone who brought, employed, or harbored the excluded would be punished. This exclusion clause was incorporated into Oregon's Bill of Rights. Two years later, when Oregon was approved for statehood, it was the only free state with an exclusion clause in its constitution.

~

When I was living in Columbus, Ohio, a friend asked me where he might move next. I had been talking up Oregon's virtues and Portland in particular—*but are there black people there?* After I hesitated, he laughed politely and said, *Yeah, that's what I thought. I'm not interested.*

There were black people there—we both knew this—but I knew that wasn't what he was really asking. He was asking if he would feel welcome, if it was a place where he could feel at home. Embarrassingly, for the first time, I faced what I had long suspected but typically dismissed as *just the way things are*: that despite its reputation for tolerance, inclusion, and progressivism, Oregon was predominantly comprised of white space, and that white space became the tabula rasa necessary for rewriting the Story. For it is impossible to inhabit the Promised Land without also inhabiting the framework that created it. After all, we are not so different from the early settlers *who saw themselves as makers of history but seldom perceived they were locked into the historical fabric of which they were merely threads*.

The exclusion laws had done their work. By the 1860 census, the state of Oregon had 52,465 residents, a population that included only *128 Free Coloreds*, *197 Indians*, and *no Asians*—a point likely noted because of the small but present Chinese population in California at the time. These early migrations resulted in *blacks in the Pacific Northwest fac[ing] a special and common problem—maintaining their existence in an area that was increasingly hostile to their presence*. The black or African American population in Oregon has hovered around two percent for the past few decades, in contrast to an estimated thirteen-point-four percent in the U.S. overall.

While Burnett may have abandoned his particular white utopia over a decade before Oregon was granted statehood, others in the region would not give up so easily. Oregonians continued to resist progress each step of the way. White emigrants drove Rogue River Tribes out of their land in 1852 and 1853 through horrific waves of violence. The state did not repeal its 1857 exclusion law until 1926. The KKK once had the largest Klan per capita in Oregon with its reach extending to numerous mayors' offices and even the governor's office. Oregon voters did not ratify the Fifteenth Amendment regarding black suffrage that was nationally passed in 1869 for ninety years. At first, they ratified the Fourteenth Amendment regarding black citizenship in 1866, but two years later they rescinded the ratification for fear of *Negro equality* and would not ratify the amendment again until 1973.

Today, despite the political and cultural diversity within various regions of the state, Oregon is nationally recognized as decidedly blue; home to pioneers in environmentalism, lovers of nature; tolerant, progressive, secluded, unspoiled.

~

The summer after high school graduation, a few friends and I heard about a spot on the South Santiam River, about fifty miles outside of town. A dark rock a bit larger than my bedroom jutted out fifteen feet above the water. Leaping, we surrendered to the water as it yanked us under, clapped through our bodies like we'd been struck, then delivered us, shivering, onto the smooth slabs of rock below. Eventually, too hungry and dazed to stay any longer, we drove home in bikini tops with the windows down, feeling like life had only just begun. We did this often—a few times a week—it's all I remember about that summer.

One Tuesday afternoon in September, still radiating heat from a day spent in the sun, we stood in front of our televisions unable to look away—bodies jumping, again, towers collapsing, again, again, again—but it broke nothing in us.

We didn't know those people, didn't recognize the skyline or how it had changed. We didn't need history because we had the wilderness, our spot on the river, our own futures unspooling before us.

~

In April of 1851, the leaders of the Santiam Kalapuya Tribe took up negotiations to remain on their traditional territory between the forks of the North and South Santiam Rivers. They were willing to sell everything surrounding it, but *their hearts were upon that piece of land*, one tribal leader explained, *and they did not wish to leave it.*

Congress did not ratify those treaties. American settlers *complained that they did not want to live among the Indians.*

In 1855, one large treaty was signed with The Confederated Tribes of the Willamette Valley. The new Indian agent agreed to Alquema's (Chief Jo) Santiam Band of Indians cultivating part of his land claim along Thomas Creek for four years or *until the said Indians shall be removed according to treaty stipulations*. But a year later, Alquema (Chief Jo) ended up moving to the Grand Ronde Reservation about fifty miles northwest. By 1860, nearly 2,000 people had been removed to that reservation and were expected to produce food for themselves but without the necessary seed supplies or equipment for the clay soils of that region.

They did not know it would end like this, in which *promises were made [...] but many times never followed through, as the promises were simply inducements to have the tribes remove willingly.* They didn't know that erasure—of their lives and land, but also how those losses came to be—would become the most indelible part of their homeland's history. In 1869, Alquema, Chief of the Santiams, responded to the latest Indian agent lecturing the tribes about western medicine and education: *We do not see the things the treaty promised. Maybe they got lost on the way. [...] Maybe you are a good man. We will find out. Sochala-Tyee, God sees you. He sees us.*

~

I fly over the land going seventy miles an hour on the freeway. I remember four teenage girls at a river named after an indigenous tribe massacred by diseases brought on foot and banished from their land by strangers wielding plows dragged behind the straining haunches of oxen. Oblivious to the world. Thinking we are on the verge of everything, knowing nothing.

The giants in the land are dead, and wherever I look the possibilities appear endless. To the east are the Cascades, to the west the roiling Pacific. You can still watch the mountains turn from pink to blinding to ice blue. Trees remain rooted along volcanic rock like aliens walking the face of the moon. Eagles nest along the gorge, and the scent of sagebrush gently mists across the high desert. In many respects, the Promised Land is alive and well—but it tastes bitter now. Too much has been buried.

Soon it will be winter. I could veer right, take the Santiam Highway all the way to the river, peer over the edge of that rock—it would be desolate—then kneel.

I could, but it is not so simple as that. And what then?

A preordained route, the interstate makes it easy. I allow it to funnel me north instead—just as the exit approaches, it's gone. I reassure myself: no one knows where or how to begin. And yet—I know—we must. I've driven this stretch of land a hundred times, and then a hundred more, surrounded by the scattered fragments of Burnett's *civilized* vision. But the air changes early tonight, the glare off the signs feels like a warning, and as the rain thickens, I strain to see.

~

Even now, deep ruts from the Oregon Trail are still visible in all six states. Imprints in stone and on grassland where the earth was so worn it will not allow growth again.

SPICE GIRL

Fierce Sonia

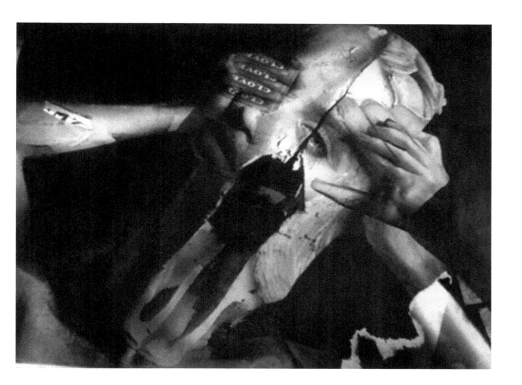

ORPHEUS UNDERWATER

Jasmine Throckmorton

for Peter

No light reaches the bottom of the ocean,
but I started out, awash with easy confidence.
You were right behind me, after all.
The dusk of your fingertips
hadn't yet been swept from my skin.
Over the roar of pressure in my eardrums,
I could still hear the heated whisper
of my name from your throat.

Towards the surface, shades
hovered at the edges and hid,
darting away like schools of fish.
Sea spider, glass sponge, brittle star,
I hoped the names would reach you.
Angler fish, gulper eel, vampire squid.
Are you with me? Are you
keeping up, Eurydice?

I kicked my feet and pushed
apart the great ocean wall.
Fangtooth fish, wolf-fish, viper fish, lantern,
my brain chattered like a lunatic, but above me,
something brighter shimmered.
My lungs throbbed, all longing
through the moving gloom.
Air air air. Light light life.
Was that the surface there?
I turned to ask you.

BAD NEWS

Jasmine Throckmorton

> *Responsibility is keeping the ability to respond.*
> —Robert Duncan

My friend and I catch up as she blows smoke rings
through the air, and I imagine my words
passing through these hoops to reach her.
Immigrant families are being separated at the border.

Through the air, I imagine our words coupling.
Her brother suffered a stroke and may never walk again.
Immigrant families are being separated at the border and
my classmate died last week from lung cancer.

Her brother suffered a stroke and may never walk again,
while she worries she might be asexual after all these years.
My classmate died last week from lung cancer
and I am away, drawing sweetened tobacco into my throat.

A friend will have surgery to remove his brain tumor.
When it rains, it pours, and today the world is dark
as I draw sweetened tobacco into my throat.
I invoke car crashes as I drive home.

When it rains, it pours. Today the world is dark.
The taste of smoke coats my tongue, where the night
is warm. As I drive home, I anticipate crashes.
Baby bats are dancing across the sky for their dinner.

The taste of smoke coats my tongue, and the night
holds me. I climb the stairs slowly to my bedroom
under baby bats who dance across the sky for dinner,
but my lover is here, sleeping in our bed.

He murmurs and a tremor runs from the floorboards
through me. I've passed through hoops to reach him,
sliding into cool sheets, sinking next to his breath.
Smoke rings widen and waste around us.

WHAT I DON'T KNOW ABOUT LOVE

Tianli Kilpatrick

1.

On the weekends I don't drink coffee, sometimes just to see if I'll survive. I didn't go to the hospital when you flatlined. There's an apple on my kitchen table rotting. I took out the trash last night and left the apple behind. The law of conservation of mass states that matter can neither be created nor destroyed. I was states away when my dog was put down; saying goodbye over the phone is not a hug. You never saw a cardiologist; you knew you had a heart problem. I once kept a snowball on a plate in the freezer. Mom threw it outside because she didn't have room for waffles. I collect soda tabs, wine corks, keychains. You retell the story of how you were dead for thirty seconds. I keep a tally of how many times.

2.

When Zeus released two eagles to encircle the world, one flying west and the other flying east, they met in Delphi, marking it as the world's center. I only buy hand soap with fish engraved on them. I dreamed I made friends with a blacktip reef shark and named her Layla because it's the Hebrew word for night. Ravens mediate between life and death, friends with the lost souls drifting in liminality. Ravens croak and crows caw. Odin's Huginn and Muninn were ravens, not crows. Fish become soap, become clean, never fully used. Love is synonymous with consent. According to the laws of thermodynamics, the sum of the world's entropies create a central zero. Sometimes I imagine waking up in an animal's body, tonight a flying squirrel with little paws to hold things or a nightingale with an inquisitive call, tomorrow a whale shark unafraid of going deep.

3.

They say the heart is the container of happiness and whatever overflows still resides inside the body. Hollow love is me standing above a grave dug too shallow for me to join you. The red-checkered blanket we've wrapped your body in takes up too much room. A poetry professor once told me never to use the word "love" in my poems. *It's vague,* he said, *tasteless.* But I am still learning not to be afraid of this word; pain is not a side effect of love. In my after death checklist for my best friend, I've instructed her to go horseback riding, to tell that guy I still love him, to burn my journals and roast marshmallows over their flame, to remember me.

4.

I flirt with Death, but I'm not serious. If I wasn't a writer, maybe I'd be working with horses full time, maybe I'd be working on a snorkel/dive boat, maybe I'd be doing something else I have never done before like studying law or playing with pyrotechnics. Macintosh is my favorite apple. The desire to die can be addicting, but so can the will to live. It all comes down to a choice. I don't question the writer's job, I question my ability. The inside of a sea urchin is orange and spongy. I thought myself immune to the helpless kind of fear. When my mom tells me she's suicidal, living at a graduate school 1,085 miles away has never been harder. I love the crunch of biting into a mac, the way it fits perfectly in my cupped hand, the way my teeth grind against skin, against teeth.

5.

There is nothing wrong with loving pain. The bottle cap warms in my palm as the sharp edges print Venn diagrams across my skin. I still play on wooden playgrounds when given the chance; I don't have to pretend to be a kid. Trauma is a science; it intensifies memory to make it feel ever present. The first playground was built in 1859 in a park in Manchester, England. At some point we all go through a crucible. Some people come out changed, some people come out dead. But there are some that don't leave. Some sit in the flames and learn to love the fire. Some stay because it's easier to embrace the pain. Playgrounds originated in Germany as a platform for teaching children how to play correctly. I am a student of trauma. I let splinters live under my skin until they decide to leave.

6.

The gravitational force at earth's center is zero. I light a candle in my apartment, watch its shadows dance across the wall. It jerks its body back and forth to music only it hears. I welcome the pain in my neck from staring too long at stars. Popcorn is not even the first ingredient in popcorn balls. The flame flickers, then is still, then flickers again. I know that nothing anyone ever does to me can be worse than what I do to myself. Gravity spins everything with mass in the universe and I forget that we too are spinning. Fire dances in glass-strangled freedom, a self-feeding star that never sees its shadow.

7.

I can say "I love you" in seven languages. Let us do more than talk of Michelangelo. The emergency number in Norway is 4-1-1. I've called it. *Te amo*. Professor Moriarty asks, "Staying alive. So boring, isn't it?" *Je t'aime*. I once danced around the kitchen with the Halloween candy bowl upside down on my head because it made my mom laugh. *Ani ohevet otcha*. Language halts me. I have to pronounce it, let it twist my tongue into shapes it does not know. Σ' αγαπώ. Horses love by grooming each other. It's true otters hold paws to keep from drifting away. *I love you*.

8.

In high school, my friends and I sharpied the word LOVE across our forearms in green, black, and orange: the colors of depression, suicide awareness, and self-injury, according to the Active Minds and the American Foundation for Suicide Prevention websites. There's a specific darkness in the back of a movie theater where the light from the screen shines off everyone's face in the same way. We drew butterflies on each other's wrists to keep us safe. Jumping out of an airplane at 13,500 feet is like swimming over open ocean. Sharpie wove through our scars creating erasure poems across our arms, poems we rewrote each time they washed away, each time different, each time more permanent.

9.

I hold myself accountable to the sea gods, to Poseidon, the hippocampi, to Enki. I wonder if whales and dolphins have gods. I wonder if the sea urchin god judges his children based on their spikes. The ocean can kill in countless ways. Swim diagonally out of a riptide. I wonder which god was born from the humpback whale's bubble net. A box jellyfish can kill a human in two minutes. I want to read the story of Seth and Loki in the same room together, who would come out alive. I wonder if a reef builds itself to teach juvenile fish how to play. Each time a male pufferfish creates his sandy crop circle, a god is born. I've seen the green flash but not the northern lights. Shrimp have the power to break a human thumb, but they don't.

10.

Love is the nicker from horses when they see a friend, the way their nostrils quiver, lower lip loosens. It's the daintiness of a red-bellied woodpecker trading food with his mate. It's walking in the rain because your friend doesn't want you to see her cry. Love is the wolf whine, ears back, head tilted, but love is also the mourning howl. When we brought you and your new pacemaker home from the hospital, our home adopted the smells of betadine and dried blood. I hear love in the sound trees make when they scrape together. I see it in the intimate way waves can be both gentle and angry with rocks. There's fear in love too. Fear that the next time he touches me, he won't be gentle.

THE OFFERING

Jerri Griffith

HOW TO EAT A POMEGRANATE

Brooke Matson

Don't think about the consequences.
Let the primal need to know
fill you with salt. You will carry its tight
belly in the pocket of your heavy coat
for three days, embrace the weight

of the question—a ripe confession,
a reticent guest. I know
you'd rather have a simple task—
a fruit with a softened peel, a puckered cheek
that yields to a dull edge.

But that's not why you're here.
If this is sacrifice, don't dilute
the amplitude of the act.
One muscled blow
will sling your skin with magenta.

When you begin, an absence
will open at the back of your throat
like an astronaut entering space feels the floor
fall away. Don't hesitate.
Use your hands

to scrape the seeds like answers
to your tongue. You will lap
jelly from your palms, bend your fingernails
backward with asking. Do not be ashamed
of the bold carpet stain—

its red, relentless proof.

IMPOSSIBLE THINGS

Brooke Matson

*It is impossible to spontaneously create quark from vacuum, but yet it
happens all the time.*
—Dr. Maciej Lewicki

There is an 83.2% probability

>   webs of mycelium have eaten
>   your nerve endings
>   and detritus curls like leaves
>
>   in the nest of your aorta. You lie
>   beside your father, twenty years
>   and two feet of earth
>
>   between. Mary comes every Sunday
>   to lay flowers and say three words for me.

There is an 11.4% probability

>   you sit beside your father
>   outside the dimension of time. He taps
>   a pipe on his bottom teeth,
>
>   takes a pull, and galaxies emerge
>   from his exhale. Black holes hover
>   about his head, the bold scent
>
>   of tobacco. *What is the nature of darkness?*
>   *Am I unborn?* The words form
>   but cannot escape before
>
>   he opens a book. Thin sheets of scripture

fan in frothy waves of the sea, whales
cascading between his fingers. He grins

and you fall in, your sea-grey
eyes open wide.

There is a 3.6% probability

your body escaped by train, a torn
one-way ticket in your breast pocket.
The carriage rocks

back and forth, bullets over the gold-
green tapestry of India at the speed
of light. A woman

wrapped in the landscape
uses the tip of her finger to mark
your brow with vermilion

as if something entered there. As if
something escaped. She turns
to steam as the train leans

on a curve, leans into sweet grass, jasmine,
colors that vanish as you think their names.

There is a 1.8% probability

your blood has given birth to begonias
everywhere it fell: in the woods where you scraped
your knee as a boy, behind the football field

where your mouth tasted his knuckles,
along the dock where ropes cut lines
in your palms. The red lips

chew their way through the loam.
They open. They have things to say.

There is a 0.01% probability

you are a great blue whale in the Pacific Ocean
culling a seam of morning krill.
You swallow a barrelful, pulse

your larynx like a drum,
surge skyward.
Near the coast of Washington,

a woman wakes to that sound, cold
in a strange bed, thinking
she heard your voice.

AWKWARD PHASE

Arrabella Proffer

CELLS

Sean Hickey

Earth dwindled behind them, and with it their fears and desires and ties of love. Let me leave my sins behind me there, one murmured at the window to himself and his god, looking back at the planet with its worlds of blue sea and brown upthrust land and white spiraling clouds above. They were headed for the spiritual front lines in their twelve individual cells that would orbit the planet at the frontier of space. The void streamed past them with nothing in it by which to discern their own movement. All they had was the hurtling sensation in their still mortal frames and the receding view of the planet, if they chose to look back at it. Each ship had already split off from the others hundreds of miles ago, and now there was no sign of them. The twelve monastic cell-ships exhausted their precisely measured fuels and drifted into their final orbiting altitude, a common and precise distance between them as they formed a protective ring around the planet, a band of angels interceding on behalf of the sinners below whose world stood on the verge of ecological crisis and nuclear war.

They were from many countries and many faiths, and they had shaken hands and bowed and touched foreheads at the launch site in gestures of respect and friendly brother and sisterhood. And now each was alone, as alone as had ever been humanly possible. He (and, in two cases, she) was adrift in no country, with only his thoughts and his God and the stars that could never be counted. Most had brought books, but two had not even those. That thought terrified the people below. But truth be told, the monks themselves were not wholly without fear, either.

They broadcast into the cosmos their prayers and rituals, their chants and the fruits of their meditations, their awe and wonder, their wishes for peace and ecological stability and Buddhahood for all sentient beings. But piggybacking on those signals were undesirable transmissions, ineradicable static: enormous pride, timidity, loneliness, doubt.

I am the first to go into space to pray for the salvation of mankind. My name will be recorded in the history books. I am the closest man to God.

There is no one now between me and God. I feel His presence everywhere. I cannot escape it, as I could on Earth. There is nothing and no one to hide me from His gaze, to make me forget. He never stops watching. He never stops watching. My every heartbeat. My every breath. My every thought.

Everyone I have ever loved is thousands of miles away, on a planet I am cut loose from. Layers of atmosphere divide me from them. If I were to drop towards them now, as I wish to, I would burn to ash. Have they forgotten me?

So many stars, so much space between them. So much emptiness, and for what? What could it all be for? If God is here on Earth and in this cell, is he also in Alpha Centauri and the Horsehead Nebula and distant quasars and red dwarfs and the billions—trillions—quadrillions of asteroids orbiting them? And if so, why?

Alone in space with no one to keep them sane and offer a sense of normalcy rooted in taken-for-granted human interaction, some were overwhelmed by the feelings and desires that existed within them, now unchecked by any external control. Others experienced a frightening loss of these same feelings and desires, the ones they had associated with being human. Out there in the void it all seemed tiny and remote and meaningless. They floated in zero gravity without effort, achieving feats that had come to the holy men of yore only through ascetic training or divine blessing—now these powers had been given to them by mere rockets. It was a miracle, and it wasn't.

The lands below watched the night skies for them, sent them prayers and admiring letters, and bimonthly shipments of supplies. Soon only the supplies were remembered. Events progressed on Earth and the holy aspirants at its outer rim were by and large forgotten.

They endlessly circled the Earth, and the Moon circled them, and they all circled the flaming Sun. They aged. Grew set in their ways. Talked to themselves until they had made a friend of their own voice, or came to hate it.

One smuggled himself, after many years, aboard the cargo vessel that was returning to Earth after delivering his supplies. But the unmanned ship had no atmosphere of its own, and oxygen swiftly ran out. The supply staff on Earth found, among the untouched, unmoved boxes, a withered creature in robes, its dead eyes rolled back in its head, as strange to them as if it had been some alien stowaway.

When this news broke, people remembered again for a while, maybe raised their eyes to the sky once that day.

The rest were still out there, somewhere between the heavens and the Earth, alone with the terrible strangeness of the stars and of themselves.

CLOUDED CHASM IV

Emma Arkell

FAMILY AND A FEW CLOSE FRIENDS WON'T THINK MUCH OF IT

Alyssa Jewell

And really, theirs was all the love there ever was needling
        through
the cedar trees that evening before the night barrel rolled

into its shortest hours and the forests fattened with new
        seeds cut loose—
the fruit of last summer's conflagration and cones of wild
        lupine flaming up

through skeins of fallen spruce trunks gone to black bark
        gone to wind
then eerie shine. All that deadweight wood would have
        carelessly passed

into another realm had it fallen unto the currents of Lake
        Michigan
yet now rests among the twenty-seven remaining glaciers

near Browning, Montana where I stop
to use the bathroom at the Subway on the Blackfoot
        Reservation,

pay for a Diet Coke because it doesn't seem right just to pass
        through
and not say anything. I should say nothing and everything.

My own muddy path turns back just above the glass
bay where in thirty years, avalanches will stop churning

its lucid waters into the shade of blue I saw in the eyes of
   someone
that mirrored my own so closely I had to turn away. I am
   ashamed

I have been pining for another life: one where I don't want
   so much
that isn't mine, one where I'm not offering up an
   uncomfortable amount of myself

and first memories, accounts of strongholds washed out to
   sea, anecdotes
of impossibilities and the miraculous turned over into the
   receptive light

of a few friends out of a need to find someone who
   understands, and mostly, I fear
understanding—the attachment it brings and the wonder:
   the sharp intake

of breath when you round the corner and the world is fully,
   in that moment,
a black bear cub scratching through the earth, undoing

sixty pounds of wild berries to satisfy the day increasing
into the mountainside at an alarming rate. In that moment,
   your world

is the gas station in your old neighborhood burnt up and
   glorious in the dawn,
is ferns and columbine sewing their summer shadows over
   the hillside,

over another animal's home, and this, now, is only as far as
   your own eye can see.

BEARDED MOTHERS

Robin Gow

I want to look at us in the company of other bearded women.

Your mom has a beard. Will you end up like that? Brett Asher asked me on the first day of second grade. I felt the urge to cover myself. I toyed with the zipper of my teal sweatshirt, pulling it up to my neck.

From as early as seven or eight I was aware of the obligation we have to shave—to become smoother & touchable. I already had hair on my shins. I sometimes pulled out a strand or two as an exercise of maturity or curiosity. The white root on the end intrigued me.

No, I don't get that.

I don't remember exactly what I said after that, but I know I made a joke about you. I felt guilty about it afterschool when you set two bowls of stew on the counter for Billy & me. Red potatoes, cubed beef, thick carrots, onions. I dipped a potato roll in the broth.

Is there a part of a girl's body that should be allowed to grow? To be wild?

That night I inspected my own face in the mirror, analyzing each follicle on my chin & cheeks. There was, of course, hair: soft & light like the fur of a newborn animal, mouse, downy corn husk, the gentle side of the Velcro.

There was always evidence: foam in the downstairs bathroom sink. The scars across her lip & cheeks. The shreds of toilet paper she'd stick to her face when she was done. We never spoke of it. We've still never spoken of it.

Darwin & his contemporaries have several ideas about why women might grow beards. Ambling, on the hunt, they traced

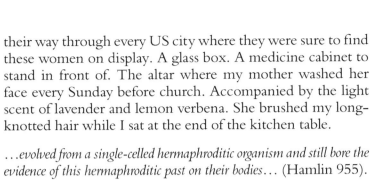

their way through every US city where they were sure to find these women on display. A glass box. A medicine cabinet to stand in front of. The altar where my mother washed her face every Sunday before church. Accompanied by the light scent of lavender and lemon verbena. She brushed my long-knotted hair while I sat at the end of the kitchen table.

...evolved from a single-celled hermaphroditic organism and still bore the evidence of this hermaphroditic past on their bodies... (Hamlin 955).

I am twenty-two & only one month ago did I learn that we both have PCOS (Polycystic Ovarian Syndrome). One of the prime markers of the disorder is the growth of facial hair in females from a young age. I wonder how many other bearded women have had it too. I wonder how many of them didn't have words to articulate the pounding fists beneath their abdomens. How many wondered what could be wrong with them—why God gave them beards.

It explains the surgery you had last spring that you didn't tell anyone about until after it was over. It explains the months we spent silently together bleeding week after week after week.

Often times people with PCOS will have irregular cycles, missing months & then having periods that can't find an ending. The sentence. A run-on.

When I was younger, I never had the courage to ask you if there was something wrong with me. I didn't talk about it. Like most aspects of each other's lives, we have somehow inhabited the same space without speaking of it.

I don't tell people that we're both writers.

You taught me where we keep the green plastic squares; how to hide them in your sleeves so the men in the house don't notice us. How to ask for more without asking for more. How to wrap yourself in toilet paper. Wash the razors out in the sink, leave the dull heads in the waste can by the toilet.

I still feel guilty sometimes for not being your daughter.

There were two instances where we painted each other's nails: 1.) You made mine look like watermelons. You had worked all day & in the dim light of the kitchen still found time to paint my small pink fingernails. 2.) I was too young for nail polish & we spilled a primrose color all over the stones of the back porch. I learned what nail polish remover was & that I hated the smell.

One of the prime subjects studied by these biologists at the turn of the century was named Viola. A sketch of her from an 1877 book entitled *Archives of Dermatology* depicts a regally dressed woman with a full-on beard. It's lush & its curls mimic the vitality of the spirals of brown hair pouring from her head. The beard goes past the scope of the portrait, out of frame. Her report reads *At about the age of ten the hair of the face began to grow more vigorously, the cheeks, chin and upper portion of neck showing an abundant production.* I find magic in this. I want to touch it. *Is that weird?*

It has been a long time since I pressed my forehead up against your face. This is not something grown men do with their mothers. Should it be? I'm thinking of you holding me in the tired rocking chair that still waits in my old bedroom. The back of the chair has an inscription that reads "On the birth of my granddaughter, Sarah."

For good reason, not all transgender people feel comfortable letting you know their birth names. I do this as an act of intimacy & because that's still what my mother still calls me.

I love these bearded women in the sketches because, despite being cataloged like animals, they have found a way to make a living out of their ability to grow hair. Does anyone do that anymore?

Another image from an archive of PT Barnum's *Circus* depicts Annie Jones. The poster reads "La Veritable Femme A Barbe" *The True Bearded Woman.* There have existed very few women able to wear a beard. I want to know if this woman was proud of her beard. I think I wonder this because of how much you resent your own. Shave close to the skin. Shave on Sundays. Before work.

A beard means something different for me now.

Even before I started taking testosterone I could grow one. It became something I could hold onto. A fragment of stereotypical manhood. I know that I needed to think of my facial hair like that back then, but I want to think of The Beard differently now. I want to think of beards as motherly, for us.

Annie Jones, from the *Circus* Poster, is most well known for being an advocate for the "Freaks" section of Barnum's Circus. I feel awful having to type out "Freaks" because she spent the majority of her professional career trying to eliminate that word from the circus world. I see her sitting in the trailers of the traveling shows, maybe, perhaps telling a story to the rest of the group. I imagine her as a writer like us. A mother.

If you Google-image-search "Bearded Women," the first search suggestion is "PCOS." These stories are interlocked.

Only this past summer did I dig more into what PCOS even really is. The body making alien—distant. Surreal. I think of our ovaries like two moons. The medical images of polycystic ovaries covered in cysts resemble the faces of planets. I prefer to think of them like this. It makes them less malicious, less impending.

I attended a session about hysterectomies at a transgender health conference this past summer. All I could think about was you. I wanted you to sit with me. I wanted you to tell me I would be okay even if I took out the parts of our bodies that we share.

I see us walking on the surface of these moons.

Three-fourths of Transmasculine people have PCOS.

The physician tossed out the statistic in a long spew of others. I wrote it on my thigh in ball point pen. Three-fourths.

I wanted to remember to tell the three-fourths to you. As if, now, maybe now, you could understand there was something chemical to it.

But then, of course, there's you. There's all the bearded women. If not chemical or medical than what is a body?

You know the gravel road? The one where last year they

planted soybeans & the year before they planted wheat? The road we would walk down when I was in middle school & still had a round face & long brown hair with knots in the back. This is now the surface of a new planet.

There will come a point when both of us will have to have our ovaries removed. PCOS often can evolve into cancer—the cysts can become painful—volcanic. When the doctors peer in at them I look away. I don't let them show me images.

I see them as mauve in color. Gentle. Can we now, though, can we now just take a moment to trek across them while we still have them in our bodies?

I don't bleed anymore & occasionally I want to. I'm not supposed to say that as a man becoming a man.

I still shave, though I have been attempting to grow out the hair on my lip. It helps me pass. I hate the idea of passing as something I already am. I hate the idea that for so much of my life the hair on my face was a mark of a *Freak* and now I have stripped it of that meaning.

I'm not asking you to grow out your hair. No one could ask you to do that.

I'm asking you to look up the images of bearded women and call me after. Call me when you're driving home from work. You never call me. I should call you. I know. I know I should.

Will you search for them then?

No, not just on the internet. I mean *really* look for them.

On mornings like this when none of my housemates are home & I just have a mirror, the hair on my face feels like a relic of my girlhood.

Would you have braided mine?

Could we have traveled with a circus? A mother & daughter.

In all of Darwin's reports he hypothesizes these women as the "missing link."

This is obviously dehumanizing, but somehow reading it doesn't faze me because I already know that's how society sees women with beards.

A boy I dated in high school once said, after kissing me & brushing up against the prickly hair on my lip,

You're going to take care of that right?

I'm speaking up now, nearly a decade later. Years of dabbing blood off my face. Years of watching you put bandaids on your chin, your neck.

I'm going to take care of *us*.

Now I know that the missing link is not one body, but the distance between them.

I should call you. I should.

Hamlin, Kimberly A. "The 'Case of a Bearded Woman': Hypertrichosis and the Construction of Gender in the Age of Darwin." *American Quarterly*, vol. 63, no. 4, 2011, pp. 955-981. Project MUSE, doi:10.1353/aq.2011.0051.

Pednaud, J Tithonus. "Annie Jones - The Esau Woman." *Circus Freaks and Human Oddities*, Retrieved 27 March 2015.

YOU'RE NOT ALONE

Silas Plum

TATAU

April Alvarez

She found herself on a creaky bike, fidgeting to make the hard ripped-up saddle more comfortable, winding down the fern-lined path past houses and dogs and chickens and palms onto the main road. It wasn't far, maybe half a mile, to the white house with the red sign that read TATAU. Almost enough time for her long hair to dry. She hadn't mentioned anything to her husband, Dom. She propped the bike against the porch. The screen door hung loosely. She peered inside trying to decide whether to knock or use the bell when a man appeared in the interior doorway, shirtless, holding a giant white coffee cup, puzzled eyes in his tattooed face. He pushed the door open.

"I'm here to get a tattoo," she said.

"Make an appointment with her." A woman with a breathtaking octopus tattoo emerged as he went back inside.

It was the largest tattoo Mira had ever seen. The arms of the octopus reached in every direction, wrapping themselves up an arm, down a leg, suckers open to grab hold. The woman wore a bathing-suit top and a short wrap for a skirt; her uncovered skin was cephalopod incarnate. The tattoo was so realistic, so different from the Polynesian tattoos all over the island where geometric shapes and lines formed animals. This octopus, Mira was quite sure, could swim and breathe and take down enemies.

She couldn't pack fast enough when Dom was offered the fellowship. She thought a year in Tahiti meant she could leave all the reminders in California. In line at LAX, a little girl in line with a Hello Kitty bag banged into the backs of her knees. She felt inescapably vulnerable. Dom vacantly watched the whole episode. Standing at the ticket counter he had looked at their smartly packed matching Patagonia bags and said, "It feels like we're leaving something behind."

What, like a baby? she had wanted to say, but only nodded.

The boat was well beyond the reef, where it seesawed in the chop, its engine cut. Silver glints of mouths rose up and cut the air: the bonita were running. The water was disturbed so violently. Birds swooped down to pull up the corralled prey fish and the tuna twisted and snapped in preternatural unison. Mira was queasy. She couldn't tell if it was from the boat or the travel or the fighting fish.

Looking out over the frenzy, she could barely see the island on the horizon through the wings of the shrieking petrels. Allen, the station manager, loaded a small harpoon, pulled Dom over to one side of the stern, and showed him how to pull the trigger. Dom speared one of the giant tuna, a wild beauty. They iced it down in the big cooler that served as Mira's seat. The tuna thumped around for a few minutes. Mira became increasingly uncomfortable with the thought of the fish floundering without oxygen, losing circulation, freezing and dying just beneath her. When the sun angled on her face, she moved forward to drink some water, using it as an excuse to change seats. The guys cracked open beers.

"Are you okay?" Dom whispered.

They were jetlagged, suspended in the hot air. Blood left her face. She opened her mouth to speak, but closed it again. Allen started the engine and took off, away from the chop. They were moving so fast it felt like they were skimming the top of the water. A school of flying fish followed the boat, their silver wings absorbing more than reflecting the sun, accumulating a luminous glow the longer they coasted over the water. They brought Mira back from the edge. The island's green volcanoes emerged from the blue ocean, two giant bays on the north side, lined by the ruins of a caldera giving the island of Mo'orea her misshapen heart shape. It must have appeared exactly like this to the eighteenth-century explorers who came to witness the transit of Venus. Like Paradise.

Within a week of their arrival, rain began to mark each afternoon, binding the sun's intensity, then retreating. Mira went out on the boat with the student researchers the first week, and several times after, but she was often seasick and in the way. They were counting starfish, only she was supposed to call them sea stars. The students moved in easy unison, confident, smart. A couple started conversations with her, but turned to their work after a few questions were met with her straightforward, clipped replies. She wondered if she distracted Dom but realized half the time he didn't notice if she was sick. She imagined him on the boat without her, engaged, relaxed, blending in with this group.

"Why don't you get something from the pharmacy for seasickness? We can go over right now. They're still open," Dom offered after a particularly hellish outing where she sat on the bow heaving every time the boat stopped. "You're seasick before we start."

When will everything stop sounding like an indictment? It wasn't her fault. Their fault. Saying "they" had at one time helped. Miscarriages happen. The nursery, the fenced-in yard, the rocking chair—they were all indictments, all now rented to another couple.

"Mira?" Dom prodded and waved a hand in front of her face. "I'm here," she told him.

One evening Dom stopped the car at the breakwater on the way back from the lab. It was late, well past sunset. Mira stood with him on the dark wall. Breakers glowed in the new moonlight and washed ashore in the easy rhythm of the island. Stars reflected in the dark water.

"You should come out on the boat again," Dom said. Before she could make excuses about the seasickness or how uncomfortable she felt around the college students and even the older graduate students, he began talking about the clarity of the water. He said he often felt suspended in the sky as he fell back from the boat. He felt unattached until he was under the surface, eyes open, taking in the light breaking on the reef.

"It's like I enter a dream. It's so clear and blue that sometimes I float on the surface and listen to the water. Then I see a grid."

The grids, or at least most of them, lay out past the breakers, past the outer reef. The researchers used them to track the starfish, which weren't invasive, but periodically their populations exploded. A large group of rapacious starfish could devastate a coral reef within a year or two: they sucked up the live coral and left a bleached stone carcass. The reef could recover, but only if there was enough time and enough live coral left. Dom was on Mo'orea to count the starfish. Mira was there to count the days.

She imagined him looking at the transept, the steel rods denoting distance and equidistance, the overwhelming number of starfish. "All those starfish," she said.

"Yeah. Sea stars."

"I meant sea stars." She wanted to assure him that she had paid attention, that she knew this, knew that they were sea stars not starfish, knew their Latin name, *Acanthaster* (rhymes with disaster) *planci*, knew they were multi-legged and sharp-spiked, knew they were called the Crown of Thorns.

The water flattened. Breakers swept to shore more slowly, as if the tide couldn't decide if it was coming or going.

"It's hard not to make associations," Dom said. "Corals are stars. I can't help but think that the Crown of Thorns are consuming these little ocean lights, these stars under the water."

"Which is funny. Since the sea stars are star shaped," she said.

Dom was quiet before he spoke again.

"I'm collecting data, and I know that's the right thing to do, it's always the right thing to do, but I'm watching a galaxy be extinguished."

A few days later, Mira caved in and agreed to go on the boat with Dom and Allen to a sea-star census. Allen said they wouldn't be going out too far. They'd take it easy. She would snorkel with Allen while Dom and a couple of undergraduates took count a few meters below. Allen handed her a pack of scopolamine patches. One behind the ear tonight, and I promise you won't get sick. She couldn't refuse the kindness.

Mira's skin tingled as Allen steered the boat across the lagoon. She tried to make out the tattoos on his arms, the bands of dots and lines. Flying fish cut across their wake. Dom missed them; he was talking with one of the graduate students. Mira wanted to remember to ask why the flying fish were so close to shore. She had thought of them as adventurers, outliers, ocean daredevils, not reef dwellers. She wondered for a second if she had even seen them. She had the sense that the nausea patch kept her thoughts from connecting.

Allen stopped the boat at the fluorescent buoy marking the survey area beside the outer reef. Dom sorted his gear and went in with the graduate student. Allen grabbed a camera and jumped in. Mira leaned off the boat. There was a moment between the boat and the water when she felt what Dom had talked about that night at the breakwater, the uncanny suspension between sea and sky. When she opened her eyes below the surface, she saw the grid, the maze of coral and the multitude of sea stars. She imagined it was always a surprise to see their convergence. She watched Dom swim toward the grid and wondered if the sheer number of starfish ever dislodged his concentration, and that instead of plodding clarity he would feel, as she did now, a darkening presence that arose from the population en masse and cut her off from everything warm, familiar, earthly.

She paddled on the surface beside Allen. The feeling of suspension left her, but the starfish made her dizzy. There were dozens and dozens of them feeding on the coral. Dom moved slowly over them, holding his waterproof chart, making tic marks on a diagram. A starfish left a rise of coral and crept up another, arms feeling its way up, subsuming the coral, a skeletal trail in its wake. Dom had told her that they normally feed only at night, but when the population crested, they'd feed in the day as well. Mira imagined the starfish as a single organism, deep purple with uncountable arms, an evil to be defeated, bleaching out all life, all connection. The mind-numbing slowness of scientific inquiry was wholly inadequate compared to the rate of destruction. She wanted to grab a harpoon and stab every last one of them.

Back on the boat Allen asked if everything was ok.

"Of course," she said. "Another day in Paradise."

Allen ignored her sarcasm and motioned over his shoulder.

"There's a story, maybe it's a chant. It's about the arrival of the sea stars, how they cover the lagoon and clean it out. Then they retreat to the deep as they've done for thousands of years."

"So this is supposed to happen?"

"You can be obtuse and say everything is supposed to happen. The point is not that they show up, it's that now they show up every couple of years. Nothing recovers. It's not a cleanse; it's an annihilation. You know what the islanders call them?"

"Annihilators?"

"Close. The Destroyer of Worlds."

The baby had still been alive when they got to the hospital. After the exams, the contractions, the embryonic fluid everywhere, the devastating news, there had been a lull. For some reason the fetal monitor was still attached. She heard the heartbeat slow down until it vanished. Dom held her hand and told her she would be ok. It would be ok. After that he was silent. The monitor was silent. The waves on Mo'orea brought back that heartbeat in a primal reversal.

She took the dinged-up bike again, hair damp, parked it under the tattoo sign. She stopped on the porch and stood by the rail, listening to the breakers on the white reef. The red windsock filled. She could see the ocean through the palms.

The tattooist brought out the completed design they had come to: a circle of three flying fish, geometric in form, with curved bodies, arrowed wings and fanned-out tails, spirals and concentric curves, composed of mazes that looked like they might spin out of the circle formed by the three. The workroom was a mélange of needles, work lights, a medicinal smell. Tattoo tools were laid out on shelves and on a little table by a swivel chair. She could see the ink: blacks and blues and a bright red.

She stood in front of a mirror. The tattooist slowly sketched the outline of the design onto her lower left hip and stomach with a red pen. His hands were soft and unimaginably clean. She was shaken by his intensity. The image emerged on her skin. She nodded, not wanting to reveal the profound pleasure this brought.

He moved her to a massage table. She could still hear the waves hitting the reef. From the table, she could see only the treetops and sky reflected onto the ceiling. Music played. On her left, she could see a giant painting of a woman lying on her side, half naked, covered in an octopus tattoo. The girlfriend. A version of her.

She pointed to the painting. "What does the octopus mean?"

"She holds up the sky."

The tattooist's hand touched the indentation below her hip, and then her stomach, as if to read what he had written on it. Then it started. The pain cut through sound and smell and thought. It was not as loud as she had imagined. This will be over with in less than an hour. Her stomach flinched and contracted. She kept silent and still as he moved his hand over her again and again. She felt unnerved by their intimacy, but like the pain, willed it to dissipate.

Smoke edged by as he let a cigarette burn. From the table she could see the shark tattoo on his arm and the other tattoos on his body. His face was divided into quadrants—one without ink at all. The others held lightning, swirls, and geometric patterns that suggested the waves of the misnamed Pacific. A lower arm was un-inked. His bicep held band after band, like the ones on Allen's arm, each detailing another aspect of his identity. The places where tattoos were absent she imagined as empty quarters secured for the future.

The pinpricks from the needle gathered into a small storm, coming and going with less predictability. He swiped her stomach incessantly with the towel. The moisture accumulating was blood. Her breathing became less measured. She thought about the process, sharp things piercing your skin, tattoo rituals on the islands.

"Have you ever been tattooed with stingray barbs?" she said.

The tattooist laughed. "No. But shark's teeth, yes." He lifted up one leg replete with blocks of black, black ink and rows of triangle accents around circles of squares, a face maybe. "From the Marquesas."

"What was it like?"

He laughed. "It really hurt."

She wanted to laugh but a jab sent a white shock to her head and reset her thoughts. He wiped her stomach. She clenched her fists. She could see the little towel in the mirror, stained red with blood. She was overcome with a dank, coppery smell. She had woken up during the surgery. Someone in scrubs held a container, what was left of her miscarriage, her baby. Her doctor noticed immediately and asked a technician to put the patient under right away please. This will be over in less than an hour.

The bikinied girlfriend walked in with more towels. A prickly sting crept over Mira's skin. The octopus' head stretched onto the girlfriend's slender side and stomach, the round eyes followed Mira's stare. Three hearts were visible along her ribcage, beating as she went past. When she turned, a gaping beak threatened to swallow the world. A tentacle reached up her torso and chest and neck onto her face, the very tip of it wrapped underneath her left eye, holding her gaze in place with tiny suction cups. An octopus not only feels but tastes what it touches.

A slant of yellow light hit the mirror and swallowed the room. Mira watched the red windsock swim against the green of the coconut palms in her mind. There seemed to be time here. A clear-eyed vision that the days passed differently. She closed her eyes and the breeze reached her legs. Her arteries and veins flowed with seawater.

She was afraid to show Dom her tattoo, like it might tip their unacknowledged stalemate in his direction, and he might win something. She wore a long T-shirt to bed that night and showered after he left the next morning. Her skin was still red and irritated, the flying fish were still suspended in perpetual black. It would surprise him. She changed out of a one-piece bathing suit to a two-piece and back again, unable to decide which to wear to the beach. She had never really hidden anything from him before, but she kept thinking I'm saving this for myself. I'm saving this for myself. I'm just saving this for myself.

JERK

Arabella Proffer

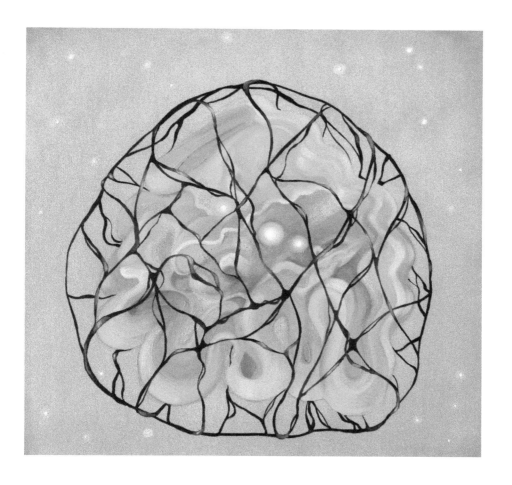

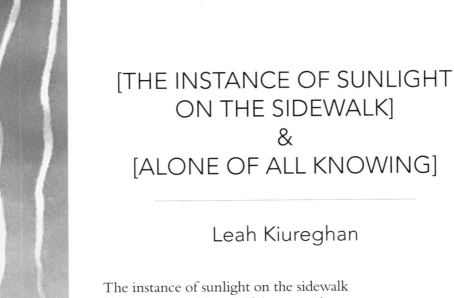

[THE INSTANCE OF SUNLIGHT ON THE SIDEWALK]
&
[ALONE OF ALL KNOWING]

Leah Kiureghan

The instance of sunlight on the sidewalk
being present still even if the ground
is darkened momentarily
with paint or, say, shadow of non-
conceptual content, say, "knead until smooth"
roughly ten minutes until elastic would not
have noticed but for your reaction when
was removed the bandage vesper light we
gracious heard the voice sometime later
on a recording patience robed fold gently

Alone of all knowing yet feeling suspicious of that
impulse and of that impulse: nothing, just _____ all
day what do you want to do first my phone I make sure
I have the feelings we have about the $55 dinner
was are they deserved far be it from me to illustrate
excess. Far be it from me but I really should hate to think
how nice you look after a long day consumed in coeval
office-share community what we have prepared together
we shall enjoy together and consume what has been
laid before us by the architect of what has yet to be created

ROE

Zack Strait

The salmon are thrashing around like knives, having thrust
hundreds of miles upstream to spawn. I wade out
into the shallow water, kicking up loose gravel to find
their nests of orange moons, tiny and round
as pearls. I bend down and scoop them up, the long strands
dangling from between my fingers. I shove them
into my jacket pockets like a burglar, splash back out
onto the bank. The game warden is already
hunting for an excuse to arrest me, ever since he caught me
skinning a buck out of season. I stagger back up
to my coupe, leave my headlights off until I'm miles
down the highway. I feel inside my pockets
for the moons, roll them between my thumb and forefinger.

AT THE CORNER OF 6TH & PINE

WLS

There, in someone's front yard
I saw a glass bowl, turned over
on a hole, with a red-brown
brick on top. In that airless
chamber, a small swarm of desperate
wasps swirled. I did nothing to end
this small cruelty. I went on walking,
not knowing what my business was.

GEE

Tracy Daugherty

In the second full year of his retirement, Bern took to visiting Trinity Church in Lower Manhattan each Wednesday at lunchtime, for the free organ concerts offered there. From his apartment on Perry, a downsized place that still didn't feel quite like home, he'd catch the 5 Express to Wall Street, clutching a lunch sack. Midday subway riders tended to be young and he enjoyed their fresh faces, lively voices. One day he admired the brashness of a girl sitting across the aisle from him. Her T-shirt, underneath her open fleece, said, "Your Boyfriend Gave Me This Shirt."

In the ads above the subway cars' dark, rattling windows, a dermatologist promised younger skin. An online university guaranteed the world at a touch of the finger. A television "reality show" exploited miserable housewives. This was the culture from which Bern had retired, and he felt more and more gladly remote from it.

Recently, one day at MoMA, he'd felt disoriented (a feeling that had persisted since then) when he couldn't find his favorite Joseph Cornell box, which had been displayed on the museum's fourth floor for years. "He's no longer a perennial favorite," a guard had told him, shaking his head. "The new, young curators don't have a feel for him."

On a bench across the street from the church, in the half hour before the concert began, he'd squeeze mustard from a recalcitrant packet onto gray corned beef. He noted the shuffle of shined leather shoes on the sidewalks. These days, the wingtipped warriors of Wall Street seemed more fretful than in the past. Nothing Bern could pinpoint. A hint of fearful exhaustion in the faces. Hunched shoulders and backs. Smart phones flashed. Empires crumbled.

Each week, at the edge of the church's small graveyard, by the wire-mesh trash can in which Bern placed his empty lunch sack, a homeless old woman stood wearing the same red cotton sweater, no matter the weather. She wheezed terribly. Bern always saved her a handful of barbecued potato chips. "Gee," she'd say. This meant "Thanks," but on other occasions, "Gee" meant something else entirely. Bern learned to read her tone. "Gee," she'd tell him, indicating dismay, backing away from a pair of stockbrokers arguing by the curb. Or "Gee," she'd say, entranced, watching a flight of pigeons from the cornice of a bank. In the spirit of retiring, of simplifying, Bern came to appreciate her eloquence.

Always, the saints embedded in the stained-glass windows of the church looked startled at the crowds streaming down the aisles for the concerts. Once the music began, the statues of the apostles behind the altar appeared to be curious and attentive, whereas moments before they were mere dead wood. The organ was amazing. An Opus 1 digital. It had replaced the Aeolian-Skinner pipes ruined by dust and debris on 9/11.

Today's performer was a twenty-two-year-old wunderkind from Germany named—of all things—Felix Hell. The program included Bach's *Prelude and Fugue in D Minor* and Barber's *Adagio for Strings*. The boy's fingers sweeping across the gleaming keys looked as pale as root vegetables. Bern read in a brochure he'd picked up that young Felix's career had been managed since childhood by his father (*there's* your bloody hell, Bern thought). The organ chords roared. A siren whined outside.

While half his mind rode the music, Bern set the rest of his awareness on an architectural problem sparked by a newspaper article he'd read while sipping his morning coffee. He still liked to imagine designing structures just to keep his brain active, though his building days were finished.

The problem was tuberculosis and the narrow-mindedness of traditional hospital design. In Africa, in Haiti, conventional wisdom insisted that thick mud walls were necessary to protect the population from the spread of disease. But in fact tuberculosis thrived in closed spaces. Perhaps a Pentagon-shape, Bern thought, or a drum-like circle, windows at opposite angles providing cross ventilation. A latticed steel roof, bamboo, maybe . . . or maybe (since he was daydreaming idly now) a curtain wall textured like the Northern Lights he'd once witnessed pulsing in southern Iceland, on the shore of the volcanic Lake Kleifarvatn. He'd gone to Iceland one autumn to study earthquake mitigation. The lake, perched on the Mid-Atlantic Ridge, drained and refilled mysteriously, year after year, from underground sources hidden deep in clefted rock. Meanwhile, reflected in the clear blue water and jacklighting the fine black sand on the shore, the aurora appeared, scattershot, among dispersing clouds, first a vaporous green band running the chilly length of the sky, then breaking up like voice-print patterns on an old oscilloscope, then flashing, dancing, spikes of brightness like a chorus line of unrobed angels, the souls of the dead; finally, showers of green and magenta loops, waves, whipsaws of brilliance certain to fall to earth, enveloping the land, its jagged, black peaks, in diaphanous drapes of electrically-charged dew.

Behind the altar now, Hell half stood, pushing aside his bench with the backs of his knees. He pressed the organ keys like a man kneading bread. Bach filled the room: musical ether in the church's tiny cosmos.

Bern had never visited Africa or Haiti but he remembered his last trip to the undeveloped world—Yemen, years ago, in his grad school days while he was researching his dissertation on architectural origins. One afternoon, the tour group he traveled with stopped to buy honey in the desert north of Sana'a. The beekeepers lived in thatch huts: palm fronds and canvas tenting. Dozens of tarp-covered boxes—makeshift hives—stood, stacked tall, nearby. To get the honey, the men lighted rolled-up burlap sticks and smoked out the bees. In brutal sunlight, in temperatures nearing 115 degrees, the beekeeper's wives stood still, draped in black garments.

Later that day, jet fighters made practice runs over the desert: first the Americans, then the Soviets.

On another afternoon, in a marketplace in Hodeida, Bern recalled, he thought he would faint for lack of shelter. Bottle after quart bottle of water and he didn't have to pee. The moisture leaked through his pores. In the streets the smell of sun-baked fish overpowered him. Vendors spread blankets on narrow walks and covered them with peppers, coffee beans, yellow cumin, and rice. Water pipes, brass plates, carpets. A severed cow's head in a wheelbarrow. Cool skirts swayed with the women's bodies. Bright yellow head wraps, blue and red scarves. The swell of odors and colors dizzied him. And that relentless heat!—along the streets, men fried prickly pears and strips of meat in steel drums (boiling grease spattering the passersby); hissing Coleman lanterns and white-hot light bulbs illuminated spices and cloths, shoes, boxes of matches, smoothed sticks for cleaning the teeth. Bern overheard a cocky young vegetable hawker quip, in fractured English, that women made poor revolutionaries because they refused to relinquish their menstrual cycles. Prayer calls buzzed from minarets.

Architectural origins. Simple shelters. Retiring from the world in the depths of the desert. Bern opened his eyes. The concert was over.

On the street, in the shadow of a steel and glass mortgage firm, in a throng of walkers shouting into cell phones, he saw several men running through traffic, dodging cabs, a Bartleby's bread truck, and a fleet of FedEx vans. EMTs—the ambulance was parked by the curb. They pushed past a busker beating staccato percussion solos on his chest with the heels of his fists. "Batter my heart . . ." Bern thought. The men huddled over a prone figure by the stone wall enclosing the church's cemetery. They shook their heads. Between their legs, a flash of red. Bern moved close enough to spot a scatter of potato chips on the sidewalk. Heart attack? Asthma? He felt weak and made his way to the bench where he always ate his lunch. Poor old woman. *Gee.* He hoped some scrap of her spirit still had reason to use that word—in awe, perhaps, of whatever she might be witnessing now. Lights in the sky. A plane passed overhead. Bern shivered. *Shelter. Bamboo. Latticed steel. The clasp of my ribs.* Gee, he thought. Gee. He stood up slowly, gratefully, and walked the several blocks to his home.

GIMME GIMME

Fierce Sonia

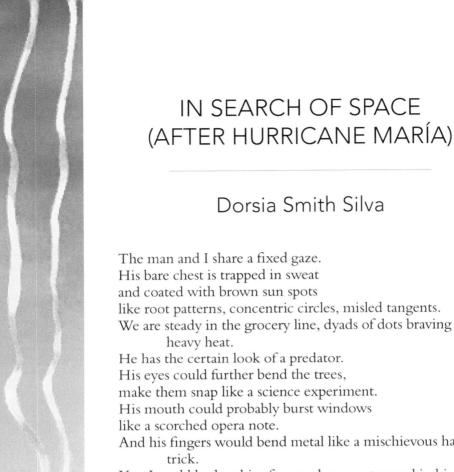

IN SEARCH OF SPACE (AFTER HURRICANE MARÍA)

Dorsia Smith Silva

The man and I share a fixed gaze.
His bare chest is trapped in sweat
and coated with brown sun spots
like root patterns, concentric circles, misled tangents.
We are steady in the grocery line, dyads of dots braving the
      heavy heat.
He has the certain look of a predator.
His eyes could further bend the trees,
make them snap like a science experiment.
His mouth could probably burst windows
like a scorched opera note.
And his fingers would bend metal like a mischievous hat
      trick.
Yet, I could look at him forever: become trapped in his
named hunger.
We inch up a millimeter and leave no quiet cracks between
      us.
Yet, we hang there in the cruelty of narrow space,
our feet holding onto our bodies trying to pull out of
      nothing,
drowning around us.

PAREIDOLIA

Clayton Adam Clark

That one's an ocelot and here's a war-
steed and this with more time could be
a locomotive coughing smoke. In these storms,
masonry paint loses more grip on the south wall
of my foundation, the moisture exposing stone
like blooms of mold. The tornado siren
began its blare an hour ago, and I retreated
to the basement where I keep a flashlight,
some food and water, blankets. As the earth
cycles through freeze and thaw, a basement
keeps a house from breaking, and so I pace
poured concrete, my ears on the weather report,
stopping at times to see what might be eastbound
through the meager windows as if I could
do anything with anything I saw there but wait
or tuck my head against a wet-cool wall,
which all but feel the same. Like Doppler radar
or radio, the barometric swelling of the knees,
I sense so much more what might be
than what will be. When I emerge in the dusk,
houses stand, but the heat's fallen from the air
and half my neighbors' tree lies in the street.
I wave to them and point at the terrible machine
of clouds that passed, the purple-blue shape-
shifting east faster than I can make out,
and point to the orange near-monochrome
steadied behind me. I don't see above us what
colors took shape between because I join them
in the patient dragging of a treetop from the road.

LEECHES

Clayton Adam Clark

After hunting mussels from shoreline rocks,
my brothers and I pinched leeches
from our legs while our catch boiled
on the fire. The three-toothed parasites
tugged at our skin, released, and then writhed
on the embers where we flicked them.
One clamped onto my thumb before it went,
an effort I admire and also confirming
for my fear of anything beneath the surface.
Even sautéed and salted, the mussels
weren't good, but we'd taken them so we ate
all we could and fed all we couldn't
back to the dark, green water.

BLACK ACRYLIC ON CANVAS

Ora and Benny Segalis

POLYHEDRAL CATHEDRAL

Peter Schwartz

The die-cut paper sat in the attic at the farm for more than twenty years. Sat in the dark. Forgotten. But then found, and assembled, in precise angular fulfillment of the cosmic law of eternal return. Crags canted and sloped like dolomitic spikes, edges of a dream denoting polyhedral passage from one destiny to another.

The die-cut paper resembled a covenanted ark. A cathedral for geometers. This would be the stuff of mysteries, of course. The fashioning of the die-cut paper into lamps that, twenty years after the fact, illuminate the secret key, the encoded message, the hidden treasure. The fatal words, the smiting hand, the spinning gyre. Twenty years too late, unfortunately, for we can now only remember what did happen, not what might have been.

~

Arpad is returning to Budapest sixty years after the fact. This decision/need to return itself (perhaps only with difficulty as he weighs 300 pounds) a precondition for discovery of the die-cut paper sitting alone, in a stack, in the attic at the farm for more than twenty years. Arpad's return, a sad/kind homecoming, embracing the physics of loss, the compression of time, the what-happened-in-between. Arpad, gigantic emotionally needy komondor (we become our dogs), folding in upon himself, a polyhedron reduced to being no more than a stack of die-cut paper.

~

In the sixteenth century, the Hungarian Reformed Church self-assembled. An exhalation, floating and unwinding and rising from its Roman interrogators at the Synod of Debrecen. These self-naming and self-identifying

Protestants, their sacred buildings housing the spirit of self-referentiality—*this is me.*

And so, these Protestant churches housed the individual. A new kind of human. Self-creating. Self-doubting.

And so, to fully separate from Rome's cross-hatched symbology, Hungarian village churches adopted the star. To beacon from the pinnacle of the spire their blessings and their curses as children of God.

~

In the nineteenth century, enabled by new copper and zinc fabrication methods (a new means of production for tower spires), aspiring churches could select a star polyhedral from zinc factory catalogues offering a wide variety of tower spires. Primarily the rhombicuboctahedron, although not without a sampling of dipyramids, rhombic pyramids, and truncated square pyramids (the pyramids technically not polyhedral, just cheap knockoffs, geometric forms attached to a spheroid center, lower-priced items in the zinc catalogue).

Protestantism then, even in Hungary, self-assembling village by village, like stacks of die-cut paper lifting and folding into each other, solids emerging from surfaces, faces meeting in pairs, edges meeting at the vertex, resolution of all space into a single dimension, a dense unifying moment, the vertex a pivot.

~

Leonardo's radiant polyhedral illustrations for Luca Pacioli's *The Divine Proportion* (1509), included a stellated octahedron, simplest of the five regular polyhedral compounds, a three-dimensional extension of the hexagram, formed from two centrally symmetric overlapping tetrahedral polygons, with fractal potential.

But we owe it all to Kepler. Who represented the universe as a series of nested polyhedra on which the planets rotate. Who named Leonardo's stellation the *stella octangula.* Who also stellated the regular convex dodecahedron, for the first time treating it as a surface (a gram), not a solid.

This is what Kepler noticed. By extending the edges or faces of the convex dodecahedron until they met again, he could obtain star pentagons. And from the regularity of these pentagons, which Kepler also recognized, he constructed stellated dodecahedra, which concealed the central convex region within the interior with only triangular arms visible. Not a sphere! Not a knockoff. A geometrically regular polyhedron!

~

Leonardo anticipated $C_{60.}$ 600 years ago. C_{60}. Welcome to the Fullerene Family! (In common parlance) the family of Bucky Balls (and other Bucky things)!

C_{60}. A polyhedron, of course. A truncated icosahedron (think soccer ball) with sixty vertices and thirty-two faces (twenty hexagons and twelve pentagons where no pentagons share a vertex) with a carbon atom at the vertices of each polygon and a bond along each polygon edge.

Buckminsterfullerene is the most common naturally occurring fullerene molecule. With philosophically significant emergent properties, indicated by unusual optical absorptions in thin films of carbon dust (a.k.a. soot, geometrically perfect dirt). With solid and gaseous forms of the molecule detected in deep space, Buckminsterfullerene is one of the largest objects shown to exhibit wave-particle duality. C_{60} dissolved in olive oil nearly doubles rodent life spans. It is possibly also useful for photovoltaic applications.

~

Arpad was an OG of solar photovoltaic technology who explored the physical properties of light (photonics), the conversion of light to electricity via the photovoltaic semiconductor. His specialty was thin-film conduction—in which we take starlight, heaven's pinpricks, stellated energy of infinite scope, condensed via tetrahedrally bonded solar cells—possessing exceptionally high light absorption coefficients.

Thin-film solar cell companies included Nanosolar (now bankrupt) and Solyndra (now bankrupt), leaving alive only spiritually dead First Solar with thin-film technology dependent on cadmium, a super-toxic heavy metal extracted from zinc. A new means of production, yes.

The polyhedral cathedral. Antoni Gaudi's Sagrada Familia. His polyhedra in the church towers spawning a new class of hollow carbon-cage molecules. Gaudi, in the latter stages of his own design journey, returned to more formal expression. *I am a geometer*, he said. But he lived in the details. Each architectural moment unique.

Philip Johnson's Glass Cathedral sanctified light with its free-form polyhedral skin defying geometry, the tent meeting reborn to serve the theatrical broadcast ministry, The Hour of Power, of televangelist Robert Schuller (now bankrupt). A simulacrum of Great Awakenings, including a spillover parking lot where drive-in congregations might listen to the sermon from car stereos. Philip Johnson's own antiseptic (formerly fascist) conservative politics here oddly implicated in the service of empty crystalline perfection.

~

Yes. The die-cut paper sat in the attic at the farm for more than twenty years. Sat in the dark. Forgotten. But then found and self-assembled through some inner compulsion. Was it an obedience to hard-coded instructions? Or to divine imperative? No matter. What matters is our urgent will to emerge from (not into) a light. Each polyhedron glows, warmly, from within. Alight. Pulsing with different hues and intensities.

We are singularities. Cathedrals unto ourselves. With facets and edges and vertices that allow us to connect and merge. We join at the vertex (our dense unifying moment). We pivot toward each other, without self-effacing, each of us illuminated by a grace of our own making.

~

Arpad, in Budapest, under the starlight, nuzzles his komondor.

TILT

Emily Marie Passos Duffy

Pelvis—archive of hospital bed and matted pubic hair—
fever scaling a mountain and burning, volcanic, from the
inside out. Ilium, ischium, and pubis make the face of a
butterfly pinned down. A place that sinks below sea level
with weather changes. My mother says, "I've never been
raped" and proceeds to recount a date she went on. In bed,
she remembers she said "no." He did not stop. Afterwards
he said, "what are you going to do, call the police?" She
didn't call the police. And, neither do I. Each time, I
think, I must have done something to deserve this. The
flesh   between and slightly above never quite lies flat—
ossa coxae frame a small   canyon that also rises out
of itself. During menstruation, molten lava twists its way
through my insides. Often, I vomit from the pain. Once,
pulled over to the side of Germantown Pike and threw
up beet juice into a plastic bag. It was red, purple, liquid.
Contained in an image is a husk of essence—the excess light
emitted and refracting. Held the bag in my fist. An image is
shucked, shed, cast off. It is a reveal, a removal of something
in excess. And if the image is thrown   off, what
remains? A map pulls back   a sheet, showing the world
to me. What is the distance between the pelvis and things it
shares space with? What is the distance between throwing
off and covering—a striptease rewound, a snake re-enters
its skin. Irrevocable, suspended like something nude,
something   obscene, something comfortable.

MANOR HOUSE

Arabella Proffer

HOTEL RZESZÓW

Dean Barker

He'll brush a speck, a surprise, January fly, from the top left of the page, gently, but leave a delicate smear of blood there, a dash no more than his thumbnail in length: cause enough for him to wait before writing his next sentence, then to berate himself and his drunk-dramatic reading of the haphazard.

Too drunk too soon. Too soon. Too soon, so drunk."

He'll turn from his own slap, twice. A lightning punch from the other hand will loosen teeth. Tears will astonish him.

~

The afternoon's bigos and a *po turecku* soup of coffee grounds will have him lift a buttock, innards bloated. (Dinner before dark at a round table of strangers in their overcoats, Joseph in and out of an icy draught: theatrical curtain across the restauracja door licking at his kidneys with every entrance and exit, every automatic *bon appetit*—"Smacznego"— muttered in passing, and acknowledged by the foreigner only, the first few times. Spilled condiments and ashtrays. Back on the meat if not quite the smokes. A trail of opened rags, wringing wet, for the walked-in snow: stepping stones from the door to the kitchen counter. "Smacznego.") Joseph will stand (clear his bowl and appear to thank it, rise from his stool) and find his balance. He'll stand at the window of his hotel room with the Monument to the Revolution—a landmark known locally as The Great Cunt: brazen, church-shrinking grey lips rising to the eleventh floor, to a pair of sharpened horns—holding him steady, giddy, head swimming after the first shoulder.

On the trudge back to the hotel after dinner, after shopping for vodka, chocolate, and apple juice and, almost overlooked, sticky tape (caught without the correct Polish and embarrassing himself at the kiosk, once at the head of a lengthening queue. "Sel-lo-*tar*-per? . . ."), Joseph will pass a largely vacant galleria piping music onto the street, playing a song he'll mutter as final words around six hours later.

If everybody had an ocean,
Across the U.S.A.,
Then everybody'd be surf-in' . . .

The sky livid, heralding new snow; old snow dirty and granulated, frozen underfoot.

. . .You'd see them wearing their baggies,
Huarchi sandals, too . . .

Eyes narrowed by the smile behind his scarf will be tearing.

~

Joseph's participation in "the next morning" will be limited solely to his presence, the puzzlement and hushed-up humour it'll cause. Corporeal weight and bloody mess of him remaining a party to tomorrow, no doubt about that in his mind.

He'll study his phrasebook, write a sign for the bathroom door, for tomorrow's chambermaid (blundering in on Joseph, sign or no sign. She'll pinball herself back out into the hall, summon a man or two from the nearby stairway to Klub Wenus).

Nie wchodź, the sign will read. *Zadzwoń na policję.*

~

Heavily pregnant, Sara will return alone to their rented apartment. She'll wheel her suitcase from the lift, gasp from an unborn kick as her key enters the door. Pulling off her coat and hat she'll notice the wooden roses in a jug of jelly beans and call out his name, expecting Joseph to be there, to appear from the next room, slightly dishevelled after a nap.

She'll see the block of C60 cassettes standing by the jug and the carved flowers.

~

"Welcome home, misia."

An inhaled fleck of saliva will start a coughing fit he'll not edit out. "Hope sea air's helped. Sea air and Babcia-to-be's secret remedies!" Cough-splutter. That'll split her sides wide, get a big aul belly laugh out of her.

He'll pause the tape to cough good and hard, get the croak from his voice. Pause released he'll wait an age. "Tell her there's no shame in this. Not for her, or for you. For no one other than me."

"Tell your mother to keep both of you close." He'll leave the room to be on his feet, to find something that hopefully won't break his hand or be broken by it.

All he is capable of saying will have been said. What more to say? There will be nothing left to say. Pity yourself but, please—*please*—shut up now. Shut up.

His every recorded word is re-recorded, sometimes over and over. Sometimes an hour's struggle omitted entirely. Finished confession chopped between exasperated sighs and sighs of relief, from strangled rage to a bitterly ashamed basso profundo in the crackle and hiss of a few millimetres. The vanity of the whole enterprise will sicken him. He'll consider leaving nothing, no explanation. Let them imagine what they will—his wife pulling apart every cassette after holding herself together long enough to listen but not comprehend. (Alone with their unborn child: "If you are *sick*, I should be *with* you!") She'll collapse, reduce to a tangled heap a confession compiled over months—hearing herself on more than one occasion in the background, arriving home and, in innocence, ending that morning's distillation of banality.

"Stepping out now's helping only way I can trust myself to help—help you, help him/her inside you."

She'll bludgeon herself in the belly with a tenderising mallet, in some fashion lose their child very soon after she's pushed and pulled out.

~

Stop. Rewind. A prolonged, chipmunk clearing of the throat the cue.

"Welcome home, misia."

Record/play . . . .

The last cassette's final twenty-nine minutes and fifty-seven seconds will capture where they lived, unspectacularly: a wildtrack of twelve floors above busy Ulica Krakówska, the recording-level needle barely twitching.

Joseph will wake and fall flailing from his chair as the tape-recorder buttons snap up. He'll eject the cassette and find a pen, write *31 december 99* on side two.

A bottle of less than enough vodka will be hacked free from the refrigerator-freezer compartment. He'll remember, just in time, to replace the telephone's receiver and the telephone will ring almost immediately. Sara. Of course. No panic in her voice, phoning home from home.

"How are you?"

They will speak for over an hour, avoiding trouble, the more or less safe ground of the coming baby the best of their conversation. At midnight each will hear fireworks some 700 kilometres away, in the other's location.

"So, Happy New Year, Mr. Walker."

"And you. Pani Walker."

She'll pass the phone to her parents, despite Joseph's objections, though he'll be charming, inescapably, his childlike Polish having it no other way. He'll exchange best wishes with Mamuś i Tatuś and even apologise for his absence (if only for something to say, something within his ability to articulate). The line will go dead after Sara's father, rather than passing the phone back, hangs up by mistake (forfeiting his second three fingers—the nalewka decanter confiscated, locked in its cabinet; soured Mamuśia taking daughter and cabinet key off into the kitchen). And that will be that. Enough.

The receiver will be left off the hook again, in case Sara should try to call back. (She'll blame Sylwester 2000 switchboard overload and soon quit trying their number, not wanting to keep her folks up.) Joseph will drink from the bottle, leave the landlady's displayed shot glasses undisturbed in their dust. Framed religious prints they'd promised would remain on the walls will meet on the balcony—a doe-eyed baby Jesus top of the stack, snowed on, snowed under by first light.

~

Checking in alone and without luggage Joseph will find himself mistakenly granted the discretion of K floor. The experience on offer above, on the highest floor of the hotel, will make no secret of itself. From every K-floor door a business card stamped with 'L is for Love'—words set behind a real lipstick print—will hang in a plastic sleeve, an A5 punched pocket, each personalised, tagged mischievously with a distance in feet and inches—Klub Wenus a mere stretch of hall and a sentinelled flight of stairs away, open for residual business the night after 1999.

Joseph will have his pick of rooms made ready after a late start on last night's abandon—the smallest rooms, understandably, the rooms tackled first. Room K47 will be tiny and overheated. He'll sit at the bedside table, barefoot, bare-chested, pen in hand. He'll scrub his beginning indecipherable and begin anew, do drunken battle with disgrace under his breath and skin and throw the first attempt at who he is/was, a few words why (and a shortlist of names for the baby), over his shoulder. He'll eye the next bottle of vodka but see reason, see himself waking on the floor to the chambermaid's knock. "Slow down," he'll say, slowing down. "Sloooow down. He'll rise, sway the few paces necessary to pick up the crumpled page, take it, drop it into the waste-paper basket— positioned curiously in the middle of the room ("Did I put that . . . there?") as if to catch a leak from L floor's bordello.

~

The bathplug will be the wrong size, a sink plug.

Fuck. Fuck. Fuck.

He'll stare from the bed at the telephone.

Fear of being sniffed out will keep him from dialing downstairs for help. Should room service catch a whiff of it, the scent of his intention will surely give him away, scramble the unwanted to the unwanted rescue. (These people are *trained*—likely on t'yous already.) *Emergency-service sirens closing in, the hotel chaplain—with professed poor English but perfect German—will sermonise through K47's barricaded door, take prompts po angielsku from spectators in the corridor, from its stars, a clutch of Klub Wenus girls in coats and stilettos, drawn down by the buzz.*

Joseph will take the initiative and pull his boots on, pull them onto bare feet.

Galeria Amerika. Europa Dwa. The opticians on the corner, the post office. Cross the street . . . . The hardware aisle of the Non-stop SuperSam will reward a twelve-minute totter with a choice of three identical universal plugs. He will buy all three, euphoric, and eight cans of overpriced stout and retrace his steps, landmark by landmark, to this very spot (and find himself still here, stripped to the waist, umming and ahhing. Dozy prick).

~

Everyone walks like a drunk on the ice.

In that case, you'll walk straighter than straight, lamed by a wildly jarring grace, guaranteed to rouse wolves from a warm van.

To head off now, to set out across the center of town in the snow in Joseph's state (shaking his head before he knows it—movement in the dressing-table mirror catching his eye), will be risking arrest and the drunk tank. (Joseph apprehended waiting for the last-encountered pedestrian crossing to turn green: waiting, swaying just a touch, not jaywalking across the empty road to the hotel but putting on a display of cautious obedience, gloveless, beer and three bathplugs in a wisp of a carrier bag (the beer paid for twice—super suspiciously without protest—on account of no phrasebook and no till receipt on returning from in sight of the hotel for the plug/plugs). All in jeopardy, in all likelihood. Fucked at the finish line.) They will hose him naked into a corner if they pick him up, find only Polski złoty in his wallet (offered, accepted) and fine him all of it for carrying no identification. His address will genuinely escape him but he'll give them his name several times, each time slurred a little differently. A smug reveille at his cell door—*Gooed morning, Yosef Wowker*—will mean Sara, despite everything, has reported him missing, or the hotel has surrendered his passport. The thought of a morning after, of a family reunion (to duelling typewriters, Sara's pain and silent questioning—meeting her eye from across the police station office), will bring Joseph to his knees. Kneeling, he'll meet his consternation between twice as many apple-juice cartons on K47's dressing table.

The Non-stop SuperSam, in any case, like the hotel bar, will be closed—is bound to be—and Joseph will sneer, nixed, and fall flat on his face on the bed.

He'll spring back up, raise a toast to Safety First! and chug down a whole litre from the carton, juice streaming down his torso. His feet will lever his boots back off. He'll force the plug for the sink into a plughole bed of grey toilet paper, holding it in place as the bath begins to fill. Bottle number two will be taken for comfort's sake. Joseph will thump its upturned base, break its seal on his way to piss, piss hands-off once out and aimed, and, glancing back to check he'd *remembered* after all the fuss, all the fun he'll clearly be having, piss a short rumble off target.

N I E   W C H O D Ź
ZADZWOŃ NA POLICJĘ

Buttoning up, he'll spin round to take the sign by surprise (affixed with chewing gum after all that, the kiosk mime act) and find it still there, nice and straight, straightforward—quite possibly a commendable effort; Polish a wilfully difficult language.

~

Steam from the filling bath will creep above the bed. Plumes of mist swirling at the open window will conjure up a row of indoor icicles—thick bars by morning. He'll empty his bladder where he lies, magnified. He'll see himself crossing the sick Wisłok from the Russian market with a lighter step, with a bargain straight razor found among unbundled bric-a-brac. (The widow behind her stall impassive as Joseph tested it on the heel of his hand.) Adequately drunk, he'll open his right arm, unfussed. No ceremony, no grief. The left he'll cut deeper, pushing through tendon, thanks to the plough/field inversion necessary not to bleed above the waterline. Blood will tumble in on itself in slicks and smoke. Joseph will close the tap with his toes. The Siren song from upstairs—*disco polo* without pause since his arrival—will finally give up the ghost, just as he turns an ear to it. His right arm will go into spasm and, urged on, thrash about of its own accord for two, three seconds.

"*That's* the spirit. *Get* in there."

The water will settle. Then he'll notice, at his leisure, a clump of pubic hair turning slowly above the plugholes . . . . The razor, gripped tight, will have slashed a hip and gouged a notch below his navel before clattering out of reach, snapping shut on the—now wet—bathroom floor. He'll realise how close his cock came to butchery and a sense of self-preservation will shake him, will flood his gut and throat.

~

If it isn't to be like this, it will happen, most likely, on the spur of the moment, without privacy or certainty. An uglier imposition.

~

Chest-high water will take shape as it darkens, wicking away Joseph's color from scalp to Adam's apple. Mirror-tiling directly ahead and behind him will now need to be avoided, the mist receding, each tile down to the same corner. His first heart attack will be seen out with barely a ripple. He'll stifle his own death rattle, hearing the thing gurgling up, comical, turned into a chuckle after farted bubbles. Bubbles will wreathe his waist, and Joseph will laugh, fingering empty space, blood coursing to white tiles. (Forgive me carelessness but there *is* a damn sign on the damn door—on the wrong side, granted.) Bottle number three (bottle four requisitioned by a shaken hotel manager in the afterlife) will be located, lifted. After almost tipping it over, fingers cut loose from muscle will lift bottle number three to Joseph's immediate satisfaction. "Bet res y'lifen tha." Not a word passing pale, tautening lips, but the whole hotel will be silenced, cocking an ear. "Bet *best* y'life— fin smear a life . . . . Add tha blag bead y'strin a pearls."

Bloody water stopped with vomit and feces, paper, the hair and scum of previous bathers, will have drained ankle deep—the plug finally plugged. Joseph's skin will mimic the tidemark and the matter he sits in. Head back, sobered up, *this* is how he'll be found: peering into his reflection behind and before the taps, his every miscalculation's same outcome shunted nose to tail for his simple perusal from the bathtub.

SPRING

Beatrice Szymkowiak

Are you there?	How long since & till mold blossoms
I hear you.	gnaw I was here
Listen. Can you whistle?	carved into walls with a broken tooth?
	Again against
Wet & round your lips.	window a swallow
Wet & round your lips.	bangs. Inside my head
Wet & round your lips.	its red ingrown hiss—
	[lapse]
Now collapse	
your lungs into a pinhole	
and breathe through	Needles
eroded teeth	piercing my jaw
into a whistle.	

THE TROUBLE WITH KIDS THESE DAYS

Silas Plum

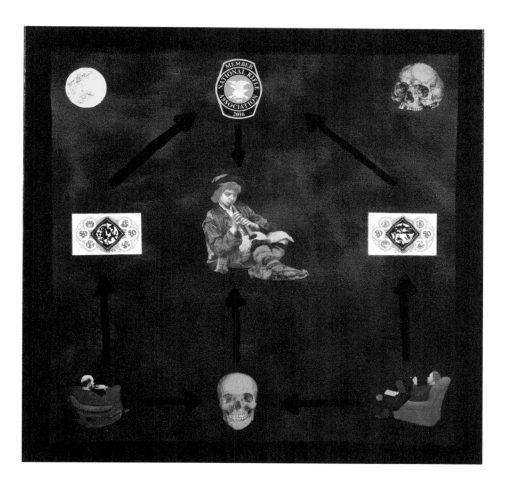

#42

Brian Gard

She paces the punk ramparts of Stark Street
with mythic strides. He said she used to be shy.
It was a Parisian moment if there ever was one.
A slight scent of what was rotting rose from the harbor,
blown like scraps of bloody foam under her long gaze.
Later she surfed at sunset. She was the only one
and the water was pink, like the first ripening
of the raspberries, that confusion in the far corner.
"What is there to learn from time," she says,
"except that it passes——I learned that in Egypt
but it satisfies no one." Her eyes hold you in her arms,
that occasional trick of the muses:
"You are determined to have an antecedent," she says,
"I, on the other hand, understand presentation."

THE SILK MOTHERS

Mackenzie Bethune

I'm thinking about my own mother as I lay my children down in the incubator in the nursery. I can see their tiny bodies writhing beneath the filmy layer of the eggshell. We separated the black shells from yellow a few hours ago. Hal and I got into a fight about what to do with the ones that didn't make it. He wrinkled his nose at them and said we should sell them. *To who?* I asked. *To science. Or the weavers. I don't know.*

It was like the fight last week about the incubator itself. Hal has seen home videos of himself nestled in an old model. Nothing like the swaddling my mother put my siblings and me in. The fire she kept burning in our room every day until we began to hatch.

The fireplace here is electric, Claudia, Hal said. *You have to be practical.*

There are only two black eggs, so I gather them in my arms and take them on a drive out to the forest. They ride in the passenger seat the whole way there. Every so often I reach out and touch them. Cold little rocks. I bury them next to my brothers and sisters who never hatched. I wonder if my mother cried when she sprinkled dirt over their blackness. Did she look past the shell at the rotting soup inside? Did she feel the urge to eat them, reabsorb them in her stomach where they'd sat just hours before? I've seen programs on tribes who practice this. The women live longer there. I pat the grass back into place and say a prayer. Then I brush off my jeans and head back to the car.

I still have memories of my mother. She had skin that shone a milky purple in the dark of our nursery, like a nightlight. She cleaned the hard clumps we couldn't reach after we fell out of our eggs and gave us each a bath in her own milk. Then she fed us leaves she'd chewed, mouth touching mouth.

I have jars of pureed leaves in our pantry. They start on the bottom shelf as a fine mush and work their way up to the top rows where they are hardly crushed at all. I showed Hal the different labels, but he'll probably forget. He bought me one of those machines that helps you chew them up. *Every bit of energy saved counts*, he says.

I'm napping after the burial. The canopy around Hal and my bed is pulled tight. The light from the windows is blocked out.

Claudia, says Hal.

I'm not really asleep but I want to pretend to be.

Claudia, Hal repeats and he pulls back the curtains. I blink giant black eggs out of my vision and see a woman standing next to Hal. She is small and round and has large breasts that I'm sure are full of milk.

This is Sarah, he says and before he can say another word I am up, grabbing her by the arm and pushing her out our front door. She falls back but her wings sprawl out before she hits concrete.

What the hell? he asks me.

You know, I say, but Hal doesn't hear me anymore. He just sees what I saw in my own mother at the end. I am reflected in his big black eyes and I turn away. Back to covers still warm with my body wrapped up inside.

Hal works as an architect downtown. Right now they're working on a bigger sylvatoreum for the pupa ceremonies. A few weeks ago he took me to see how it was progressing. Gentle light from lamps made to look like stars. Sturdy trees made from steel with hooks to hang cocoons from. Plastic grass that was green like the fertilized lawns in our neighborhood. No dirt, no flowers, no birds. Hal smiled at me as I stood against the backdrop of a realm he had created. *Someday our babies will grow their wings here*, he said. I nodded and then excused myself to the bathrooms where I threw up into the shiny, sterilized toilet in a boxy new stall.

He keeps bringing home big jobs like this. And even bigger paychecks that he uses to buy gifts for me and the eggs. The silver necklaces and *homespun* dresses made my head dance when we started dating. The wedding dress from a boutique and the pearls woven into my hair. The diamond I wear on my left hand that cost more than my mother's house.

He ordered something online the other day that I promised I would try out. It comes when he's at the office. The UPS guy widens his eyes before he floats back down the sidewalk to his car. I run my fingers over the hollows of my under-eyes and cheeks. Through my remaining wisps of hair. Some come out in my hands and I let the white fluff fall to the ground.

I pick the package up and take it to the nursery.

Hello, babies, I say, ripping through layers of tape and cardboard.

My mother moved us to the city after my pupa ceremony. I was the only one who survived the unveiling. A hawk got into the sacred ground and ate all the others. That was one of the last ceremonies they held outside.

It's a sign, my mother told me that night as she combed my hair and oiled my new wings. I winced. They were still so new. Then we went out to the forest and buried my siblings who had died in the cocoons to my right and left. Mother and I had extra helpings of leaves that night.

I pull the silver cords and boxes out of the package and press a button. It glows green and I begin to hum. Then I press another button and hear the hum echo back at me. I try again, this time singing. I press play again and a ghost of my mother escapes into the air. I look around at my babies. *Did you hear that?* I imagine the gurgling noises they'll make for Hal as he feeds them and cleans them and tucks them into their cradles. The cradles are still at the carpenter's. He has to put the final coat of paint on them. We cancelled the two for the halflings, but it still takes time to make seven cradles.

We could do this with the cocoons, too, Hal told me a few weeks ago. We were standing in the carpenter's shop, watching him sand down the headboards. I could feel them inside my stomach, bumping around in sacs of fluid.

What if I crack them? I had asked my doctor at the last ultrasound. She laughed at me.

Just like I laughed at Hal. I watched his pupils scan over me. I had more hair then, more fat in my middle. He pulled me into a hug right there in the middle of the carpenter's shop. I stepped back and put a hand on my stomach. *Careful.*

I sometimes wonder what my own father was like. My mother had no stories about him. Did he hum while he read the newspaper, like Hal? Did he notice small things like the soaked tissues that piled up on a girl's desk in the days following her mother's death?

In the city I met a group of girls my age. We went to a school where biology and calculus replaced the weaving and cooking courses from my old town. When we graduated they went off to colleges in coastal towns where the girls were like them. *Like boys, you mean*, my mother said. She was fading, her head shiny and bald at the dinner table. I crushed morphine tablets into the leaves I chewed with my own mouth. I stayed close to home, caring for her in between classes.

Claudia, she said on her last night with me, *never forget the silk that spun you*. Her eyes were milky with cataracts and she asked me to come closer. I took her veiny hand in mine and said that I wouldn't. The goddess took her with a smile on her face.

I leave the recorder playing in the nursery whenever my own voice gets too tired to sing. Then I sit in a rocking chair and spin blankets.

Hal comes in one day before I can wipe the silk spittle from my lips.

Are you kidding me, he asks. There are tears in his eyes.

I can't forget the silk that spun me, I say.

He picks me up from my seat with one arm and carries me to our bed. I've never liked sharing it, but he insists. He likes to run his hand over my wings while we drift off to sleep. Most nights lately I will get up after he sleeps and stand in the middle of the nursery. Today he tucks me under the covers and brings me tea. He sets a napkin beside it with my supplements. *They don't work*, I want to say. Instead, I swallow them and let him pull me close to his chest.

I get cards from my old friends often. They are wedding announcements, baby showers, pupa ceremonies for their already grown larvae. It seems I have just taken the picture off the fridge of the chubby toddler with green fluff all over and there he is, stepping into a cocoon with a nervous smile on his face. Like their mothers and fathers before them, these caterpillars would never dream of spinning their own cocoon. Their mothers gave them baths with milk bought from another woman online.

We could too, Claudia, Hal has told me a hundred times.

When we first met, I wanted all the silver polished things he had to offer. I was like the magpies that stole fairies in the tales my mother told to scare me as a caterpillar.

I go for a walk that night to a shrine not far from our house. There are giant oaks here from the days that pupa ceremonies were all done outdoors. I look for the cracked statue in the middle of them all. The goddess emerging from her own cocoon. Please, take care of them. All of them.

After Hal and I got married, I went to the doctor to talk about children.

You spun your own cocoon as a girl? she asked me, taking a vial of blood from my arm.

When I said yes she clucked her tongue and said she highly recommended adoption. Then she gave me two pill bottles. *Take these for energy and these to keep the caterpillars away.* I threw the latter away immediately.

A few months later there were nine egg sacs in my stomach.

I've seen pictures of Hal as a larva. I hope our children have his dimples. I hope their fluff is a lighter shade of green, like mine was.

Nine? Hal screamed at the ultrasound technician. *That's impossible.*

I laid back on the cot and sipped water from a glass cup. I felt my mother's cool hands on my forehead, telling me all would be well.

The reporters wanted to do an interview with me. No one in the civilized world had had a litter of more than five in generations.

The goddess has blessed me, I told them. Hal ran his hands through his hair and groaned. He never comes to the forest with me.

My friends have been sending baby gifts. Stuffed animals and blankets, onesies and dresses. All made with hands and mouths they will never see with their own eyes. I take them to Goodwill and replace them with what I have made on my own.

They start to hatch one night. I hear the cracking of shells in my sleep and I fly out of bed. My wings hit the doorframe as I shoot into the room and look at my babies crawling into the world. Hal rushes in after me and we work together in the moonlight to pull any limbs that are stuck from the depths of their old worlds. They cry as we dip them in the basin of milk I have filled with my own breasts. Then we dry them with towels and set them in the cradles that arrived yesterday morning. We name them quickly, the ideas springing to our heads like instinct.

Out of all the larvae, there is one girl. I give her an extra kiss. I pull a necklace from my pocket. I have worn it since my own mother kissed me goodbye. I put it in her chubby hands and watch her chew at it with her gums. *Protect her*, I pray. The last of my hair falls onto the nursery floor and I walk not back to the bedroom where Hal has just settled in, but to the car. My voice is trailing out of the nursery from the silver box. My mother's songs put a spell on the entire house. I drive until the sun is just peaking over the top of the forest. I park the car and stumble over foot trails I knew so well as a child. My wings curl downwards and I fall to the ground before the ancient stone statue.

I pull my legs to my chest and let the memories of them wrap around me until I am closed up from the earth for good. I have no milk left, nothing to spin into blankets or clothes. I hear a woman call to me from outside the final shell I have made for myself. I don't know if hers is a voice I've heard before or not. She pulls me gently into her arms.

UNDERWATER

J.E. Crum

VARIATIONS ON THE FINDING

M. Allen Cunningham

Here is a picture. Here is a child: scrawny boy in Sunday clothes, brown pile of hair that does not fall into the eyes as hair tends to do in descriptions, but juts and bulges asymmetrically.

A bright Sunday morning and the boy stands alone behind a country church in Corralitos, California. Corralitos means "small enclosures." The name originates one October day in 1769 when the men of Spain's Portolá Expedition—scurvy-sick, weary—rest starving pack mules in this spot while searching for the fabled Port of Monterey.

The boy is five years old. I am the boy.

No. To say I am the boy may be technically acceptable, but impossible. These memories are hardly even mine. I have questions. Can we reclaim—any of us—innocence toward our own first perceptions?

The boy stares over a low wooden fence into the apple orchard on the other side: trees upon trees in the sunlight—trees without end. Within this moment the boy senses something different. Something new. Is it because this is the first time he's ever been truly alone?

The boy decides he'll run away.

Can the act of memory work as a kind of perforation? Trace a child's outline, press with fingertips from behind, watch the image come loose in the hands.

Again, no. The boy is a piece of every situation, every background. Here: the orange shag carpet of a living room littered with holiday wrapping and toys, his fourth Christmas.

Here: a highway shoulder's ellipse of weathered asphalt and a mound of greasy white, the day he first sees snow, age six. Here: sun-bright orchards, the first time he's ever contemplated running away. Setting saturates everything.

No one sees him. Not his parents or siblings, not the many others now praying or singing inside the church. Let's not lie when we remember. No one sees the boy, most of all not I: his mute far-off undreamt of future.

The boy decides he'll run away, as boys and girls do. He climbs the low wooden fence and his feet sink deep into apple orchard earth and he sets off walking while back inside the church Sunday school begins and nobody notices he's not there. He will be gone a long time. "Lost," they'll call it.

Where is he going? Where was *I* going? Where did the boy think he was going?

~

15 October 1769. More than sixty men in the Expedition: soldiers, muleteers, cartographers, priests, and Captain Don Gaspar de Portolá himself. They are searching for Monterey, a natural harbor they've only read about. They are in sore shape—starving or sick or both, and several have recently deserted. Overland through strange rugged country devoid of game, they've come 450 miles from San Diego. They have passed through numerous abandoned native villages. Anyway, as men so fixed in their purpose, the native narratives are unavailable to them. Lately reduced to eating their own mules with a garnish of moldy flour, the Spaniards are still in quest of the elusive Monterey harbor, still dragging along. They've traveled inland after camping several days at a place they call Rio del Pajaro near the future township of Watsonville (where I will be born), and now they reach the Corralitos site. Here they behold something previously unknown to Europeans. According to their chief engineer Miguel Constansó, whose diary provides one of our best accounts of the expedition, they find "the largest, highest, and straightest trees that we had seen up to that time. Some of them were four or five yards in diameter. The wood is of a dull, dark, reddish color, very soft, brittle, and full of knots." They are looking at a grove of magnificent coast redwoods.

They call the site La Lagunilla, after a small lagoon nearby. But often on this expedition priest or superior will name a place one thing while soldier calls it something else, and in this case the unofficial name somehow lingers as the Expedition moves on: "Corralitos."

Today some locals surmise that the name derives from those redwood groves, which still grow there. As the Spaniards would have noted, the redwoods stand in circular clusters, forming numerous small enclosures.

So: "Corralitos," where two centuries later a white country church stands amid orchards. Where . . .

One bright Sunday a boy's spiritual life begins.

~

Five years old, a boy tramps alone through a sea of apple trees, deep in the pleasures of his mind. He has no thought of time. He has no other life. He's become somebody else, in a different place. This is easy because he's so very young. When we are very young we are largely insane. It is our primary business to be lost in our imaginations. Later on we become lost in time.

We're slow to understand time. To sense and reckon the passing of hours and days—this skill is not inborn. First the world is timeless: all abundance or all scarcity, an ever-recurring present. And much later, finally, we blur into our backgrounds, or they into us. The edges and colors seep and bleed—temporal, spatial, personal—image into image, layer into layer. So any story may just as well begin with the dead.

~

Perhaps begin this story with the dead. The dead are part of the setting, part of the oversaturation in every old photo. The dead are the surface against which a child's shape grows clear. Even unpeopled scenery contains them: orchard row, country highway, farmland vista. This includes the dead of the historical past.

Pen in hand, fingers at keys, my thoughts turn round and round the dead, round and round a child's first imaginative flight: hours, it must have been, although the memory survives as just a few moments, mirage-like, and maybe of hopelessly personal significance. Impossibly insular. There are large things that come so early on that later you can only believe you've dreamt them.

I can try, maybe, to extract the boy from dream, but even if I wished it he won't be separated from what surrounds him. Corralitos apple trees, white country church, and eight miles west: the vast liquid expanse of Monterey Bay. And the more definitely I locate boy in setting, wandering lost and dreaming, the more setting expands to include the Spaniards wandering lost at Corralitos in 1769, Portolá and his men unable to find the harbor of Monterey, although it lies just behind them.

First: a brief episode of purely personal significance involving a five-year-old boy in 1983. Second: 18th-century imperial exploration of the so-called New World. These things are unalike until in my imagination the landscape holds them together.

Or rather: Imagination is a landscape unifying unalike things. Let us wander in such a landscape. Isn't this our whole project—to be lost, and yet somehow to see where we stand?

~

1602, nearly two centuries before Portolá. Spanish explorer Sebastián Vizcaíno writes an account extolling the virtues of Monterey. A civilian businessman with a taste for mercenary exploits, Vizcaíno has undertaken his journey on his own dime, promised the reward of a Manila galleon in the event that he should locate an ideal Alta California harbor for the crown. Vizcaíno christens the great bay in honor of Viceroy Monterey, and describes "a noble harbor, the best port that could be desired . . . sheltered from all winds" with "many pines for masts and yards, and live oaks and white oaks . . . all near the shore." Vizcaíno wins his galleon, and nearly two centuries later the image of his ideal natural harbor still haunts Spain's imperial imagination. Roused to jealousy by Russian explorations along the Pacific coast, the Spanish crown determines to finally claim and secure the spot.

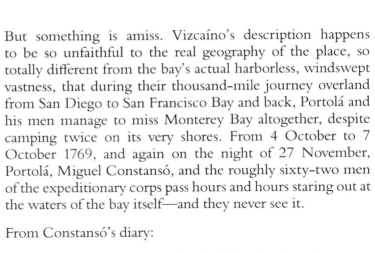

But something is amiss. Vizcaíno's description happens to be so unfaithful to the real geography of the place, so totally different from the bay's actual harborless, windswept vastness, that during their thousand-mile journey overland from San Diego to San Francisco Bay and back, Portolá and his men manage to miss Monterey Bay altogether, despite camping twice on its very shores. From 4 October to 7 October 1769, and again on the night of 27 November, Portolá, Miguel Constansó, and the roughly sixty-two men of the expeditionary corps pass hours and hours staring out at the waters of the bay itself—and they never see it.

From Constansó's diary:

"We did not know what to think of the situation. A port so famous as that of Monterey, so celebrated and so talked of in its time by energetic skillful and intelligent men, expert sailors who came expressly to reconnoiter these coasts by order of the monarch—is it possible to say that it has not been found after the most careful and earnest efforts, carried out at the cost of much toil and fatigue? Or is it admissible to think that it has been filled up or destroyed in the course of time?

The accounts of General Sebastián Vizcaíno and his contemporary historians give the port of Monterey as being 37 degrees north latitude . . . .

Having examined the whole coast, step by step, we have not the least fear that it may have escaped our diligence and search."

Being precisely where they meant to be, they believed themselves lost.

~

"One is taught," writes John Berger, "to oppose the real to the imaginary, as though the first were always at hand and the second distant, far away. This opposition is false. Events are always at hand. But the coherence of these events—which is what one means by reality—is an imaginative construction."

Description is everything, and it is more innate than we usually realize. All that we see we describe to ourselves.

And maybe while we are still young we look for ourselves in every story. Later on, being lost in time, we have the advantage of surrendering to the inviolable landscapes and lost time of other narratives.

Perhaps, while walking in an apple orchard, a small boy begins to levitate.

The coherence of events—which is what one means by reality—is an imaginative construction.

The boy is levitating. The boy realizes he did not climb that fence now far, far behind him, but levitated over it. And now, his feet pedaling aimlessly beneath him, the boy goes upward through the interlocking canopies of apple trees, through branches bulbous with fruit. Upward into soft air and sunlight, orchards ruled out neatly below, his shadow rippling tree to tree.

And soon, looking down, he can see all geography, all history, all time. Old California: its first peoples grinding acorns, weaving baskets, harvesting grasshoppers, renewing the soil with fires. And then the late-comers, the namegivers. He sees Portolá's bedraggled men, their sickly mules.

~

No one has told them that the crown revoked Sebastián Vizcaíno's prize galleon. That they hung his mapmaker for forgery. Even when faced with the actual bay, even starving, even diseased, the Expedition cannot face its own motivating error—cannot face that Vizcaíno's words, upon which the Expedition relies, are fiction.

~

California, epicenter of dream and error, was born in fiction. 1510 Madrid, two and a half centuries before Portolá: Garci Rodríguez de Montalvo publishes *La Sergas de Esplandián*, or *The Exploits of Esplandián*. It's a knocked-off sequel to the chivalrous Portuguese romance *Amadís of Gaul*, which Montalvo has translated to huge popularity. So enduring are *Amadís* and *Esplandián*, that a century later Miguel de Cervantes will blame both books for withering Don Quixote's brain.

In *Esplandián*, the titular hero and his father Amadís, while defending Constantinople against a pagan siege, find themselves attacked by one Calafía, fearsome Queen of California. This lady's kingdom is itself a fearsome place, "an island," as Montalvo describes it, "on the right hand of the Indies [and] very near to the terrestrial paradise." California is thick with horrible griffins all lusting for battle who are known to pluck men from the ground, carry them up to the stratosphere, and then send them falling. Amid the griffins live heartless Amazons who wield weapons made of the island's only metal (yes, gold). These women warriors trap young griffins and raise them for warfare in their caves, feeding them "with the men whom they took prisoners, and with the boys to whom they gave birth."

From his early-sixteenth-century letters to the Spanish royalty, written during the explorations that led him to Baja California, it is clear that Hernán Cortés fully expected to find an island of Amazons in the region.

"It may have been in derision," says one California history, "that Spanish explorers gave to a barren and hostile place the name of the fabled land of gold they had hoped to find."

~

9 December 1769. With only fourteen sacks of flour remaining to the expeditionary team, many of the men having taken ill with scurvy, two native Indian guides having deserted, and two muleteers having gone missing thirteen days prior, the Portolá Expedition, after wandering north and south, plants in the sand of the beach at Carmel a large cross fashioned of driftwood, engraved with the words: *Escarba: al pié hallarás un escrito*, or "Dig! At the foot thou wilt find a writing." Beneath the cross is buried a letter written by Miguel Costansó:

"The land-expedition that set out from San Diego on 14 July 1769 under the command of the Governor of California, Don Gaspar de Portolá reached the foot of the Sierra de Santa Lucía on 13 September . . . . It completed the passage of the mountain range, going completely round it, on 1 October and on the same day came in sight of the Punta de Pinos. [Punta de Pinos is in fact the southern-most point of

Monterey Bay.] On the seventh of the same month having already examined the Punta de Pinos and the bays to the north and south of it without finding any indications of the port of Monterey it decided to go forward in search of the port. On 30 October the expedition came in sight of . . . the port of San Francisco. The expedition[turned back] believing that the port of Monterey might possibly be found within the Sierra de Santa Lucía and fearing that the port might have been passed without having been seen. The expedition arrived again at this Punta on the twenty-seventh of the same month. From that day to the present 9 December the expedition was engaged in searching within the mountains for the port of Monterey . . . . Finally now disappointed and despairing of finding the port after so many endeavors labors and hardships and without other provisions than fourteen sacks of flour the expedition sets out today from this bay for San Diego. Pray thou Almighty God to guide it."

They leave the cross standing there on the beach at Carmel. The Expedition is a failure, though by accident they have found and christened the bay of San Francisco.

~

Hoping to purge Don Quixote's library of the books that caused his madness, Cervantes' barber and priest come upon the first blameworthy title: "This," says the barber, "is *The Exploits of Esplandián*." And the priest answers, "Open that window and throw it into the yard. The first faggot on the bonfire we're going to make."

Earlier, Cervantes pictures the readerly exertions that have ruined Don Quixote's brain, his overexposure to chivalrous verbiage like: "The lofty heavens which with their stars divinely fortify you in your divinity and make you meritorious of the merits merited by your greatness." Don Quixote's madness and the vain labors, hardships, disappointment, and despair of the Portolá Expedition desperately dependent upon Vizcaíno's descriptions—these share a culprit: bad style.

The boy levitates upward still, slung securely in a hammock of air, some invisible force bearing him higher. Years later, when the boy is a young man, he will sit in prolonged self-confinement putting down words, reading, putting down further words. This too will be a form of levitation. All that time he will ask himself: *What do I mean to say? How will I manage to say it? How, in the saying, will I banish untruth from the expression?* This is the same as asking: *What is a voice? What is a style?* And he will learn, slowly, that what characterizes bad style is not the length of one's sentences, or the use of adjectives or adverbs, or brazenly resorting to arcane vocabulary. He will learn that what characterizes bad style is mendacity. That bad stylists are careless with the truth at the heart of their subject. He will learn that a calculating mercenary lives in all of us and bad style is the failure to root him out. You can't write with something else on your mind. Having something else on their minds, bad stylists miss their own point altogether. Bad style is the failure to get lost, the failure to loosen the grip on one's own design and wander abroad in the sudden country of the material at hand. It is a failure to surrender to the disciplinary truth that no success is guaranteed, and so it's an incapacity to surprise oneself. Bad style is claiming you've made a journey which your own lines reveal you never made. In the end, bad style is always a form of lying. And lying differs in substance and quality, if not in aspect, from imaginative creation.

[Style is] sensibility and technique distinctively brought together. —Jeanette Winterson.

In the pursuit of clarity, style reveals itself . . . [Style is] an expression of the interest you take in the making of every sentence. —Verlyn Klinkenborg.

[Style is] a language as precise as possible, both in choice of words and in expression of the subtleties of thought and imagination. —Italo Calvino.

The beginner should approach style warily, realizing that it is oneself one is approaching, no other. —Strunk and White (The Elements of Style).

~

Finally, back at the church the boy's parents and fellow congregants raise the alarm. The church bells clang, quaking over the orchards. The boy hears, utterly strange, the sound of a name being called. Unfamiliar voices. Down there, very far below, a strange woman and her child stand in the orchard, waving. How do they see him up here? How do they know him? He moves toward them, confused, wind whistling across his forehead, visible streamers of sunlight flowing upward through his outspread limbs, leaves of apple trees crashing in his ears, cluttering his sight with green. Then he's standing at the woman's side and she is bending down very close.

Your parents are awfully worried about you.

She takes his hand.

Back on the ground, the boy is a pinpoint on a map, a microscopic divot on a quadrangular mass of pink labeled NORTH AMERICA. From the solar perspective, beholding the watery globe itself, the boy is not even a divot, not even a dot, not so much as a speck. And yet, from whatever unthinkable distance, in the context of whatever infinite scale, out of whatever epoch has long since been foretold, doesn't the boy shed, in some way, an uncanny residue somewhat like light?

The boy, remember, is not me. A mass of incident and impression, he is someone else's story, not yet autobiographical. He has no narrative. Body and mind the boy has been, until this moment, a dream, a person dreamt by the land itself, a creature not yet awakened to consciousness. But this is the day it happens. Look. There he goes. The land itself has seen him and all at once, a change. The boy is no longer just a dream the land is having. There is a waking and now boy and place are distinct—interwoven, blurred forever at the edges, but no longer indivisible.

How long was the boy gone? How far did the boy go? Called down, called forward out of his own native timelessness, he has learned, somehow, that despite all efforts and assertions, despite all our many small enclosures, it is imaginative structures that carry the day, that dreaming and being lost undergird our every moment.

Dig! You will find a writing.

Years later still, the young man is a father. "If I stayed up all day and all night," his five-year- old son announces, "I could watch my body grow!" The father buys a large colorful book for his son. The back page folds out and there is a clock with moveable hands. We are good heirs and good benefactors. He moves the boy's hands on the hands of the clock.

~

On the beach at Carmel, having found the Spaniards' cross, the native people, the Ohlone, bedecked it with necklaces of mussel shells. They encircled it with arrows stuck point-first into the sand. It became a shrine.

LIBERTINE AXON

Arabella Proffer

A THOUSAND KNOTS

Stacey Park

While Cat and I are restless, the ottoman rests. Cat sprints
like an olympian with no finish line, back and forth
in a three hundred square foot apartment.
Then he sleeps and eats and throws up
from eating too much Meow Mix.
Then he sprints again.

Cat has infallible truth.
The ottoman ministers catechism:
   What is the chief end of Cat?
Cat responds:
   To sprint and eat and throw up and to enjoy sleep forever.
There is this ottoman and Cat and I—
Ideology is the chasm between us.

The ottoman is covered in cat hairs;
so coiled, entangled, and complicated.
A thousand knots in a bushel of cat hair,
or so I think—I think about this one knot,

one knot nesting in my mother's womb,
a grapefruit for an ovum,
pulsating familiar pain with renewed angst.

I think about helixes of theology, philosophy,
principles, volumes, and chapters of rules.
What is the chief end of me?
I think about doctrine; I think about prayer,
my mother's health, praying for my mother's health,
if praying for my mother's health will make
   God sprint;
if praying is an opiate.

On the ottoman, Cat kneads my stomach.
We're an emblem of everyday gesturing,
I'm fine, but only one of us
needs confirmation.

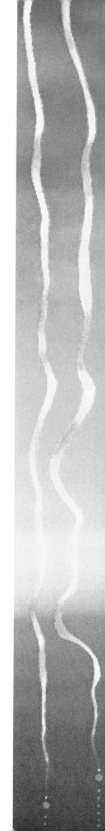

THE SMELL OF PENNIES

Rita Stevens

Behind the high fence lay a pond that bubbled foam in gorgeous pinks and greens, iridescent in the sun. The fence kept Max and Dory out, but if they breathed deeply they smelled something like the pocket change their father let them sort. They lived down the hill in a tall wooden house, the only house on its own street.

Max said he wished they could climb the fence and taste the colors, but when he dug in with his toes and clutched with his fingers he found he wasn't strong enough. Dory was even smaller and, besides, she was afraid to try. "Too bad," said Max, rubbing the indentations the fence had made on his hands. They remained outside, faces pressed against the silver wire.

When the rain kept up its battering for a long time, their basement filled and the quiet blacktop of their street disappeared. The next day they couldn't see all the flowers at the window end of their mother's living room rug, and the whole family stayed up in the bedrooms sniffing a smell of wet that climbed the stairs behind them.

"Look," Max said to Dory, the day the clouds broke up. He was standing by his bedroom window. There, in the backyard, they saw floating colors, glowing in the beaming rays, their own beauty come to visit. "Don't tell," said Max.

Two days later, after their father had once again walked to his job at the nearby paper factory and their mother had gone to buy food, they quickly found their winter boots and ran out in back to what was left of the pretty puddle they'd seen near the rusty swing set. They didn't like the taste of pink or green or even, to their surprise, Blue Moon. For a few minutes they played break the bubble, then hurried back inside and hid the boots.

And later still, in the dried-up basement, they found depleted color, patches of dusty rose and avocado. "It's like magic," said Max. They got down on their knees and put their noses close. Somewhere they could still smell pennies.

.

THE FOREST

Jeri Griffith

INTUITION

Robin Reagler

It begins in my hands.
The idea, a perfect greenness, speeds
up my pulse. I feel it radioactive
in my wrists. The point of loneliness
is to escape the living. I do not mean
to stare into this wilderness.
Above me, miles of angry
sky. Like a secret stored inside
the body's cells. Like having a crush on
the camouflaged truth. Like my mother, dying, nearly
dead, still telling me which hill to climb
and do I hear her? Am I
near her? Because for just this once
I have no doubt: when she dies
we all die with her.

CHARLIE IS LUCKY

Robin Reagler

Those of you in mountains without a dreambook
feel the ominous sequins in your eyes and are lost

A wish, feathery like
a too friendly pocket

is changing the changing
a bad landscape erupts in a pale halo

but Charlie has a failsafe plan against darkness
and has written it with footprints in the snow

Ping! The map unwraps itself
time seizes the myth of us

Ask a question

We? we are part of what
is what and real and doing wheelies in the sky

A frozen web collapses
coaxing white into the season in favor

RE: CANNON BEACH

Robin Reagler

for Ruth

A cloud reminds us to worship

says the sky. We feel

them as we walk.

Desire is

is a sharpened knife. If you

sing like a train. Hunger

Time is a pair

is a toy. Bliss, a bar

hands to tell you

and what I need

arrested by how

a single thing

all that is blue. Be the blue,

these things and repeat

Fear is a ball.

a wall. Courage

are missing your sense of place

is a bell. Talk is a goat.

of handcuffs. Sex

of soap. I've used these

what I mean (love)

(love) and I've been

we are a rock

a rook in the morning.

THE TRIAL OF MR. PINK

Silas Plum

AUBADE FROM VOYAGER 1

John Paul Martinez

Houston i am grazing   inside the deep field   only with
the telescopes   will you observe   my lilting

all i hear for now   are symphonies   the stars and tiny
sonatas   so in a few ways   i am Kepler

in a few ways   i am Chopin   have you found yet   my
coordinates   fleeting all the time   Houston

i am drifting   towards a new sun   stranding close
enough   to learn its warmth   so i melt snow

globes into comets   i am   my only shooting star   i
am   one great distance   away from home

from all the surface   fires glinting   on top of this earth
we've built ourselves   i must continue

believing in myself   like a placebo   so when i first open
like a nightshade   beneath the swelling moon

the world will notice   my plummeting signal
clear and astronomical   long and absolute

THE POWDER-MEN
IN THE TREES

Jeff Frawley

We live along the lush-dry corridor, blocks up from the Train Mouth. After school, flouting rules, we walk Akela Road. Heat splits our nostrils. Dirt browns our undies. Dogs leer and nip. These are dry-boy and dry-girl problems not suffered on the lush side. Trains rumble through the Train Mouth, met by men with prods. Crates of goods discharged. A massive chainlink fence: thirty feet tall, ten deep. Talk of electrifying it again, thanks to sneaking dry-boys. We curl fingers through its links: lush-side forest far as we can see. Branches. Dangling nests.

Cocoons. That word we've learned in eighth-grade lush-science lab. Evangelist Lab-Tech Jansen, here on a prestigious lush-side grant, brought in three cocoons in dishtowels. Furry, sticky, small as prickly-pear fruit. What's within? he whispered. Wittle powder-babies, we answered. Like grown-ups, he said, so we said, Little powder-babies. In this lab, he said, we use *scientific* terms. So we answered, Powder-fledglings— no, powder-embryos. Latinate, he said. We told him, *Homo pygmaeus vampiris.* Bravo. He slit the silk with a scalpel. Out oozed goop. He fingered open amnion, exposing a tiny face: wooden, whitened, seed-black eyes. Teeth.

He smacked our hands. Don't *touch.* Will it bite? we asked. He sighed. We've *covered* that, he said. To your desks, pop quiz. First he grabbed a pestle, ground the creature's skull. Quiz done, he dipped fingers in prayer-water, flicked. They choke if cut too early, he lectured. They *cannot* cross the fence—it's *your* fence, children, erected to protect. If they get sin inside their heads, we'll spray them, cage them, train them out into the desert. Do powder-*women* sin? we asked. He laughed. There *are* no powder-women. We protested: But you've taught us all there is to know about accountable fucking—*mustn't* there be women? Evangelist Lab-Tech Jansen, like most teachers at Savior's Reach Outpost #4, can snap from tender to tempestuous, shouting about darkness, blindness, God. But, clutching chainlink, we concur: he isn't *so* bad.

~

At four-fifteen the powder-men emerge to pick cocoons. Inching down their trees, cute as puppets. Hissing, flashing teeth. We sing the special lesson-hymn learned in second grade from Evangelist Math-Tutor Mary Vitagliano, swapping words for *powder-men*: "*One powder-man put here by the Lord up in the sky, two powder-men put here by the Lord up in the sky, three powder-men put here by the Lord up in the sky* . . ." We count twenty, twenty-five. Crawling along branches, powder-white, bald, penises like worms, pubic hair and armpit hair and chest hair black as coal. They loosen cocoons, hiss, retreat. We wiggle fingers through the chainlink, wish they'd carry us so gently. Then, our parents' cries. We whisper, Goodbye, *Homo pygmaeus vampirises*, and hurry up Akela.

At home we soak our soles in alcohol and baking soda. Hush, our mothers coo, dabbing ointment on our sores, imiquinod on bruise-like keratoses. Tell us, they say, about Evangelist Lab-Tech Jansen, Evangelist Choir-Director Olaf, Evangelist Grammarian Evaline Peebles, Evangelist Headmaster Dr. Birmingham A. Lundgren. We help with laundry, dinner sandwiches, backyard dog and goat scat. Our parents, born pre-monsoons, have insides unspoiled by runoff. They weep when Evangelist Headmaster Dr. Birmingham A. Lundgren announces that the first lush-side dry-migrant villages will be ready by graduation. But later, back home, they question: is it safe, given this news, to relinquish—as proposed by the Evangelist Headmaster—familial labor entitlement lines?

~

Our cysts are getting bigger, spurt sour-smelling pus. Don't, our parents wail, exacerbate metastasization! We giggle at these grownup words echoing what dry-boys do alone, dreaming of dry-girls. Dry-girls do it too, we've heard, but thinking about powder-men. Is this true? we asked Evangelist Grammarian Evaline Peebles. Children, she whispered, you must always, for your own sake, behave with emigrant village selection in mind . . . .

Our parents' bosses at Aztec, at Anadarzac, at Wyatt-Bellwether insist our cysts are merely cosmetic. They rattle off lush-side studies. They say, We thought you dry-siders *pray* for rain— now it makes you sick? We stay out of such debates, focus on the powder-men, on determining what older dry-girls picture when alone—ashen faces? little fingers? needle teeth? Don't cocoons, we giggle, look like dry-boy down-there things?

The powder-men, we think, can sniff our cysts. Maybe *this* is why they hiss. One day, out of nowhere, they skulked down to the ground, crab-walked to the fence. We chested chainlink. They gurgled, sniffed our legs, lipped our feet, nibbled cysts. One girl wet her pants. Others whimpered. Someone gasped, Oh God. But we dry-girls and dry-boys didn't run. We closed our eyes, heard smacking grunts. We peeked: they sucked our cysts, faces wet, feasting like cactus-bats. Their cheeks bulged with our stuff. Mouth-foam burned our wounds. *More,* we groaned, gripping fence. They shinnied up the chainlink, worked our necks and chins. We each fed six or seven. On the lush side, we've heard, we're called Snot-Skins, Udder-Legs, Eyeball-Necks. But now we were Powder-Legs, Powder-Thighs. Two guards sprinted from the Train Mouth, thwacking prods on fence: *Enough, get back, shoo!* Powder-men scattered. Come back, we cried, come back! Someone whispered, *Look.* They crawled into their trees, out along those branches, drooled into cocoons—our *stuff.* Yes, we whispered, yes. But *why?* At home we wept with pain, pinned down by our parents. Salve and passionflower sleeping snuff. They read a letter sent by Evangelist Lab-Tech Jansen: *You're dry-teens now, my children. Promise to wait for scabs before returning to that fence.*

~

Last year marked the opening of our first lush-side product-stations. One is called 7-Eleven: tree-green roof, machine-cooled air, half-stocked shelves of expensive lush-nuts, lush-fruits, jerkied lush-meats. The cheap stuff—cookies, candies, crunchers—sold out long ago. We knew a dry-boy on the night-shift, Hondo, but 7-Eleven got word that dry-boys steal for friends. So they brought in old lush-women who watched the aisles like hawks. Shift done, they returned through the Train Mouth, passing vests to their replacements, shouting *Long live Dockery-Natchez Holdings Company!* as the iron gate swung open.

Hondo got us started on the cheesedogs: cheaper than sandwiches, tolerably salty, smoky filling, digestible bread. When temperatures reached one-hundred, Dockery-Natchez Holdings Company sent vans into our neighborhoods to give away free cheesedogs, chased by packs of pit bulls. Cheesedogs make us sleepy. We dozed off in the parking lot until 7-Eleven women dumped water on our faces—their manager, we heard, forbids doze-offs.

Hondo always said, Drink liquid with those cheesdogs. Cheesedog plus a Splish cost one-ninety, lemon-lime tanging off cheese, mouth aching—*more*. But 7-Eleven sold off all their Splish. We begged Evangelist Lab-Tech Jansen: Teach us the recipe! He brought a can to lab, said, Guess. But fifteen minutes later, fed up, he said, Damn it, I'll just tell you. Water, lemon, corn syrup, baking soda. *Corn* syrup? we asked. Like prickly-pear sucralose, he answered, but better. PPS—that stuff that sweetens porridge, that fathers put in pulque. He showed us the pump basin behind our classroom trailers, overgrown with lush-stuff, a little lemon tree. The pump's the *real* miracle-worker, he whispered, but don't tell Evangelist Headmaster Lundgren.

Baking soda was easy, trained in every week. When Evangelist City-Managers learned we still clean with Blitz, they showed us what happens to items—meat, teeth, mice—when left in Blitz all night. They bought and buried cans of Blitz, passed out crates of baking soda.

We wanted to gift the powder-men for helping drain our cysts. Meat, we heard, encourages cocoons. So we sold bootleg Splish to cheesedog addicts, bought jerky with the profits. Evangelist Math-Tutor Mary Vitagliano helped calculate a price: fifteen cents. Just like lush-side kids, she gushed, rushing to tell Evangelist Headmaster Lundgren. We built a stand from baking-soda crates, crayoned the Splish logo, sold countless cups to dry-kids cramming cheesedogs. Faces clammy, lips white, they nodded off, snapped to, ordered more. In just two days, enough cash for jerky—mule deer, peacock, something called mud-boar. The 7-Eleven woman scowled at our coins so we showed her our addicts. Then, at the chainlink, we watched the powder-men gnaw. Jerky gone, they turned to us. Oily wet eyes, mouths stuffed with pus. They jittered up trees, drooled into cocoons, came back for more.

~

Dockery-Natchez got word of our stand. Businessmen arrived to jab prods at addicts, smash apart crates. Failure, one cried, to cease vending plagiarized product in vicinity of this station, property of Dockery-Natchez Holdings Company, will result in severest allowable penalty under the Lush-Dry Judicial Transference Act, section twenty-two! Two addicts were tasered. Our Splish days ended. Then, summer here, we went back to cramming cheesedogs. A friendly late-shift lush-woman, Vender Angelina Clarke, rubbed water on our lips, begged us to drink, said, Go to the chainlink, get those cysts drained before you get sick. She refused pleas for cheesedogs, three-a-day max. Food scarce, prices soaring, sun furnace-hot, we lost weight, looked like pit bulls, all sores and bones. The clinic gave dousings of pink stinking sunscreen that stung our wounds, drew flies. One night, woken by Vender Angelina Clarke, we snuck to the chainlink—never, warned our parents, go after dark. Toads thrummed, foxes yipped. Lush-moist rolled through the chainlink, slicking skin.

This was the night we learned those cocoons, filled with our stuff, light up the trees like lush-heaven. We nearly fell over. The forest pulsed blue. We leapt into fence, felt the powder-men's latch. Soon heard parents' cries. Their lantern-lit mob dragged us back from the fence. A father cried, I don't *care* what Headmaster says. Another replied, It's their *recommendation*!

We shook with dehydration. Our stuff glowed like miracles—someone said, We're *special*.

We were banished indoors, no 7-Eleven. *Always take a parent to the chainlink*. Without cheesedogs we sweated, emptied our bowels. Only drainings soothed our stomachaches and sores. Now we held hands as the powder-men sucked. Dockery-Natchez vans prowled, giving cheesedogs. What, we whispered, do they *do* with those cocoons? August collapsed like a star, blacktop splitting, pit bulls opened by vultures. Our parents walked to work sharing parcels of cardboard to block sun. We darted between yucca and oleander, pumpjack and shack. The powder-men's latch felt weakened by heat. We craved schooldays, strong Evangelist fans—at the lush-side emigrant villages, we're told, every bunkhouse will have fans.

~

First day back, we're gifted tins of marshmallow ham. The latest, boasted Evangelist Lab-Tech Jansen, in dry-side nutrition! Later that day, Evangelist Grammarian Peebles cut off our drills (To *who* we shout our praise or To *whom* we shout our praise?) and, wiping tears, said, Please, children, don't eat it *all*. The ham, whipped and pillowy, spread beautifully on bread. Who paid for this? our parents asked. We shrugged. That night we woke screaming in pain, as if swarmed by hybridized sand-wasps. The chainlink! we begged. Hordes of dry-kids arrived, parents in tow, trees glinting like diamonds. A strange airhorn from the Train Mouth. The powder-men feasted, now using teeth. More poured from the trees. Parents sobbed. We groaned in pleasure-pain. Then a man's booming voice: *Praise be to God*. We turned. There stood Evangelist Headmaster Dr. Birmingham A. Lundgren, flanked by our teachers.

Dockery-Natchez vans, the next morning, broadcast announcements: *School's delayed, let your children sleep*. Later, tins of marshmallow ham. Evangelist Lab-Tech Jansen let us eat in the lab. *You're* the lesson today, he said, scribbling notes, doling white bread. *White* bread! we cried. He asked: From where will energy for the new inter-towns come? We throated down ham. Evangelist Grammarian Peebles again stopped our drills (He maketh me *lie* down in pastures or He maketh me *lay* down in pastures?) to let us nap and spread ointment. That night, the chainlink, the airhorn, the powder-men. The next day, marshmallow ham.

~

The last thing we remember—or second-to-last—is a lush-boy in rags leaping out of a train-car.

Face grayed by coal, arms bloodied by leftover beef. We're admiring the dry-side unloaders' sun-leathered skin, muscular arms. Then someone screams. The lush-boy comes sprinting our way, shouting. But *what*? He makes it ten yards, is tackled and tased. His skin starts to smoke. We spot, just before, a thing on his rags—a patch? part of some uniform? We've seen Evangelist-history picturebooks, the rise of the lush-side, the casting out of the Trouble Boys. This one *looked* like a Trouble Boy. What was that patch—the moon? someone asks. No, says another, a bird, a lush-hen. Prod-men are shouting *Get back to the fence!* The powder-men hiss, mouths wet with stuff. The boy, or what's left of the boy, is tossed onto train as though a dead cat. Guards threaten to tase. So we turn to the fence. The powder-men latch. Not the moon, not a bird. We look to the trees. Cocoon? Lightbulb? Fruit? And what did he *shout*, that rag-boy, that Trouble Boy, that bloodied blackened cat?

We limp up Akela, desperate for cheesedogs. Doze off in the lot, wake up, throw up, head home for ointment. At night, itching wildly, we return to the fence. The next morning, Evangelist Lab-Tech Jansen, looking nervous, wraps us in his arms, smooths our necks, strokes our heads. Starts to shake. It's love, children, he whispers. Children, it's love. The pride you'll soon feel—the things that you give! *Energy*, children. Kissing to life magnificent towns. Limitless inter-towns. You're bridging both sides. Don't you see? You are blessed.

WEEKENDER

Arabella Proffer

LINESCAPE : COLLECTING VOCABULARY : REAVES, LEAT ...

Lori Anderson Moseman

living hedges   **we lay on the floor beside her**   *born thorns*
earthen banks   **we hold her shaking**   *complex sacred landscape*

cloud of jackdaws   **her mouth floods with weird words**
          oracle of HÆGTESSE
bellow used in smelting   **syntax intact**   *old tin mine's leat*

fingerprints of ancestors   **hands and knees on floor**   *power*
          hammers that crush ore
odd bleating sheep   **she rises through all fours**   *melt-water*
          glaciers' retreat

a much-worked wilderness   **she is ready**   *reaching valuable*
          islands
labor's testament   **sitting back on heels**   *Sweet Track*
          unearthed

celestial movement   **she lets us lift her**   *pot of hazelnuts*
communal effort to connect   **we usher her to bed**   *plank path*
          over peat

Reading Hugh Warwick's *Linescapes: Remapping and Reconnecting Britain's Fragmented Wildlife*
while on vigil for DeLoris Siverts Anderson who had a stroke while in hospice for renal failure.

A THIN WASH OF NEUTRAL TINT AND ROSE MADDER

Lori Anderson Moseman

The book wants me to make a weak winter sun with a cork
and masking fluid I do not have.
I misunderstand what a color pencil can do.
Too much force, plus a little spit, shreds paper back to pulp.
So, I just write lines on the cold press surface.
"Obliged" is the only word that blurs
as I dare to add more water.
"Turf a rebirth" stays firm.
The nurse claims dehydration kills most swiftly...three days.
If only I had splurged on the proper materials—
a tray with little troughs for the washes.
Naples yellow and vermillion over the whole horizon
with a number 12 brush
would make me a simple silhouette, a finished sky.
There's air hissing in the room where mother tries to sleep.
Her nasal mask out of place.
The door is closed so I cannot watch her hands adjust
the contraption made to help her sleep a deeper sleep.
Each day inching for the finishing nap.
The lesson after that: low cloud and mist
wet into wet on the mountains.
At water's edge, I'm to paint a dark mix of burnt sienna
with ultramarine. I'm to merge and soften,
to spread during the drying time.

FREQUENCY RHYTHMIC ASSIMILATION

Lori Anderson Moseman

don't just play time, blend (listen to what is already there…offer what's not)
—Will Calhoun[1]

between mid-latitude cyclones, coastlines guard consonants
watertight like a Kathlamet canoe, vowels float sun

       although there is no "we"
       we have each eaten together

back when the 1922 fire rid this port of KKK
back when labor movements took care of family
back when filet knives joined Pulaski axes and swung
side by side before hurricane simulators shook *here*

       imbalance unbearable, we fulcrums
       drum against pogroms—
       kick, snare, high-hat—time-fill tracks

rattle beside that one boat made for gathering urchins
the one that rode tsunami tides from Fukushima
to ride wakes of pilot boats entertaining brew masters

       stack of voices—copious, incompatible
       abundance—setting up the shuffle of faith

molars in an open jaw, we near a river known for shipwrecks
offer our only honey since hive collapse—our quaver tone

[1]Drumeo, "Will Calhoun – Frequency Rhythmic Assimilation," https://www.youtube.com/watch?v=oo0fYTnWqLQ.

SET PLAY

Amalia Gladhart

The crowd rustles into their seats, happy to be here. We're in the basement of the house my brother has rented from the family, a picturesque pile in the old part of town the city is trying to spruce up for tourists. Rent is a strong word—supposedly he's paying something. He does keep the place up. My grandmother lived here for years, lived alone when you'd be afraid to go out at night, when people who wanted to see the historic architecture were warned to take a trusted driver, don't linger. That's all over now, only a millionaire could even think of buying a tiny apartment. But my mother inherited a whole house here in The Cliffs. Three stories, lattice shutters, ceilings high enough to lift the heat, an unmatched view of the river. A house my brother has turned into a guesthouse-slash-cultural center, with a tiny theater space in the basement.

Going by accents, at least half the audience isn't from around here. The guesthouse may or may not be fully legal (I'm sure he doesn't have a permit) but the city loves the cultural bit. He's on the must-see list, great local color. My grandmother was private, reserved with strangers, but even she would probably approve. My brother's persuasive. He wouldn't quite lie, but he'd tell her about what goes on in the basement in a way that let her imagine red velvet drapes and opera glasses and the crème de la crème.

A woman behind me says how charming the area is. She'd been worried when the guidebook said "formerly seedy, a long-time, no-go zone." I almost turn around and tell her this was my grandmother's house, but then a man's voice next to her says the finer homes were built by the most distinguished families, back at the turn of the century, and I decide to keep my mouth shut. I try to place the accents and I try to sit up straighter, like I'm in the know. Still, I have butterflies, clammy hands. The reviews promised an emotional rollercoaster. I can't stand suspense.

Did I say basement? It's more of a cellar, dug into the rock, completely unfinished, creaky wooden stairs and a bannister more like a matchstick. The walls curve into the darkness and disappear, and it's hard to tell if the floor is dirt or cement. I wouldn't be surprised if there was water seeping out of the walls. There might be bones in the corners, rodents or worse. Not that my grandmother tolerated rodents. At least he didn't charge us for the tickets. I'm sure he considered it. But it's a family occasion, having us here.

Come to think of it, everything looks a little too familiar. The seating, the little basket full of programs, the rug at the base of the stairs.

Anything that's not nailed down, my brother takes. If someone's hands aren't physically on it, whatever it is, it must be abandoned. You don't need these chairs, do you? So now we're down here in the cellar sitting on the lawn chairs our dad always kept in the garage for summer parties. My brother's painted them red and gold, what he calls vintage style. He's so creative, sees the potential in everything— lamps, ottomans, ashtrays. Everything in the guestrooms upstairs is vintage. Or trash-picked. Or stolen.

It's a full house—twenty or thirty people. The lights go down and then up, to let us know they're ready to start, and in those twenty seconds of darkness, the actors take the stage and the audience whispers and nudges and hushes, ready for Art.

The bride is lying on the bed, feet still in those pinchy satin heels but her veil artfully draped over a lampshade for what her groom has just called mood lighting—that got a chuckle. We're going to be with these two for a while: the play follows the couple from their wedding night into old age (that's what I read in the program) and it looks like it's going to be slow, because the bride is stretched out on that midnight blue comforter rotating her ankles in those awful shoes and extending her arms over her head as if preparing to take us through each and every moment of the next fifty years in real time. She's an athlete and this is her marathon. The groom is still fussing with the set, a candle here, the bouquet she refused to throw over there.

I can't take my eyes off the comforter. Midnight blue like the sky when you're camping, when the sun's just now truly set and the stars aren't yet out. I've only seen that color on fabric one other time, and it was a comforter, too. It was my comforter. My comforter that I haven't even used. I bought it on my last vacation and put it away for winter and there it is on the bed. Some sweaty actress is grinding her hips into my comforter and the fold creases from the box aren't even all the way smoothed out yet.

I start to stand up, I'm just a little out of my chair, but my sister puts a hand on my arm. Wait, she breathes, and I think fine. Just this once. Maybe it isn't really mine. It's not like I had it custom made.

The bride sits up like a horror movie corpse rising out of her coffin (did I miss something?) but then she hops off the bed and pulls back the covers. Mr. Groom's mood lighting is sure working for her. And she's about to spread that sprayed and snarled hair all over my pillowcases, the ones that match the comforter, which are not only midnight blue but printed with stars. I can almost feel that matted hair against my cheek, as if I were the pillow, crushed and abused and out on display yet invisible as usual: a prop. The groom leers and unbuttons his shirt. Suitable for all ages, the posters said. I wonder how far this is going to go.

~

Disheveled, exhausted, they look like they've just crossed a desert on foot in their matching tracksuits, gold velour with black piping. Something really bad has happened to these people, but we don't yet know what and I don't really care. I'm looking for more of my furniture, more of my linens. The wife slams a suitcase down on the bed—probably trash-picked, the bed's about to collapse—and gets ready to unpack. I recognize that suitcase.

My sister leans in, even before I shift in my chair. Don't worry, she whispers, and I wonder what she knows. Did she come to rehearsal? Has she seen it all before? Maybe she already knows the contents are hers. She's always had a soft spot for our brother, always defends him. He's so artistic. Such vision. And with her, he might have had the courtesy to ask. She's a little older. It sets her apart.

But the careworn bride doesn't unpack right away. She sits down on top of the case, on the bed, like someone trying to force an overfilled satchel to close. *Give it up, Pandora!* the husband barks. *Everyone knows what you have in there.*

Does she resist? Protest? Prove herself worthy of that absurd mythological name? No. She bursts into tears. I recognize the actress now, a local star famous for her ability to cry on command. She's gushing, splashing, watch out for the flood. She overdoes it; the husband grows uneasy. Gingerly, he puts his arms around her. Did he just wink at the audience, over her shoulder? Is he taking this seriously? He quiets his wife, sniffles and snuffles and enough crumpled tissues to mop up an Armageddon of snot. And suddenly, it's over. Rollercoaster, right? *Ten years*—she snaps her fingers—*just like that. Where did it go?* She dries her eyes on her glittery sleeve, opens the suitcase. My sister lays a hand on my arm again, so I know something's coming.

Stuffed animals, but not the usual ones: a bat, a skunk, an armadillo. A scorpion, a rat that's almost cute. Husband and wife place them one by one on a shelf. I start to relax. The toys aren't mine. *We buried Javier*, the wife says. I've been so focused on that rat, I don't know if Javier is their son or their gardener or somebody's boss or maybe one of the pets. The woman to my left dabs at her eyes. I want to ask her who Javier is, but she's wearing the sleek black of an arthouse regular and I can't tell if she's crying from laughter.

For the best, the husband says. The wife unpacks the rest of her bag. Normal things, a sweater, some t-shirts, long pants.

And my slip. A full slip, pure silk, one I bought for far too much money to go with a dress that is probably underneath it in the suitcase, because I've had it hanging in my parents' attic. There's a beautiful cedar-lined closet up there to store clothes out of season and my brother has evidently emptied that closet right onto this stage. He must have driven a truck up to the door under cover of darkness, not that our mother would stop to question his comings or goings. He's the Artist, I'm the Good Girl; even now, they're always checking up on me.

The wife holds the slip up to her chest, smooths it against her, fluffs her hair and makes a little lip-pursed sneer toward the invisible mirror. My slip isn't good enough? She sighs heavily. *Try it on*, her husband suggests, *for old time's sake*, but she just sighs again, loud as a wind tunnel, and tosses it vaguely in her husband's direction.

I wore the dress to the regional awards reception last year. For work. I didn't win, but it's still a lucky dress, a classic. Flattering, I thought, but not to judge by the woman up on stage, who pulls the dress out of the suitcase at last like some kind of woolen snake and drops it to the floor in disgust. Her face collapses under its heavy makeup into studied despair.

Shh, my sister hisses, it's a play. Like I'm too ignorant to get that.

The husband tacks a poster up on the wall, one he had hidden under the bed. I can just make out the scraps of tape that tell him where to line it up. A poster of Venice. Just your average tourist poster—faded, torn—and no, I didn't want it anymore, I'll never go to Venice, but it was still mine and he never even asked. I plant, I save; my brother harvests.

Not Venice, the wife complains. *Could you be more clichéd?*

Awful, isn't it? the man agrees.

Like your dialogue, I want to shout. My brother's lucky there's no intermission, lucky he isn't on stage. When I find him, I'll strangle him.

~

I'm surprised to see the couple looking so old, gray at the temples and a little padding around the middle, because everyone gets fatter with age, right? I guess they didn't wear those tracksuits to the gym. We're out of the bedroom.

I don't recognize the table, that's something, but, damn it, those are my chairs, two straight-backed chairs that used to stand in the hallway, and the porcelain candlesticks shaped like happy pigs, those are mine. Did he really think I wouldn't recognize those? Did he not even care? *Not those tacky candlesticks from your grandmother*, the aging bride says. My brother must have been beside himself, thinking how well my things matched the script. Or maybe he even revised it, just to have an excuse to use them. He always teased me about those pigs.

They're setting the table for dinner, waiting for their daughter and her husband to arrive, and they get into an argument I don't even hear. I don't catch a word over the audience's laughter and the blood in my ears. It's about to gush out like a fire hydrant, I can feel it. The husband raises the sugar bowl over his head.

Of course. He has to threaten her with the sugar bowl. He's been calling her *sugar* and *sweetpeach* all night, all forty-three years of this supposedly hilarious, treacly union. My teeth ache with sympathetic decay.

Twelve place settings and all the serving pieces, gold-rimmed, translucent—the dishes really are vintage. I bought the china for myself, like a hope chest. I wasn't waiting for some fairy tale wedding. I just wanted something beautiful to look forward to. Something of my own, no Prince Charming required. I've been living with my parents, saving to buy my own place. I'm not some parasite. I just got the promotion, I just made the down payment. And now these cretins are about to start breaking my irreplaceable antique dishes to make sure we spectators understand that they're destroying their fake marriage on stage.

The husband rolls his eyes (the actor's so bug-eyed, they practically pop out of his head) and he turns a little toward the audience, so we can see how he's pawing the floor like a bull ready to charge, but then he sets the bowl down with exaggerated patience and says something steely and biting that makes the audience roar.

His wife isn't mollified.

Neither am I.

My heart is pounding two hundred miles an hour. I can't take my eyes off the woman's hand. She's lifting a plate, she's holding it like a discus. This isn't even a crime of passion. It's wholly premeditated. Practiced. She draws back and bares her teeth and everyone's still laughing but what I see is hatred, what I feel is hatred, because she's holding my plate. At last I grasp the director's logic: there's only one sugar bowl, but there are plenty of plates.

Unless they already broke some in rehearsal.

And that's it. The last straw. The thought of them smashing my dishes when no one was even looking rockets me out of my chair. This time there's nothing my sister can do or say to stop me. I vault over the empty seat in front of me—I was a hurdler in college—and thunder up on stage. Too late to catch the plate, I snatch the sugar bowl out of the husband's hands before he can hurl it at his wife after all. His forehead is bleeding, stage blood smeared where she hit him, and I do manage, in that split second, to admire their finesse, that the plate can break in the right place without cutting him for real, but then I wonder if it isn't real blood instead.

Real or not, we all have blood on our hands.

FACE IN THE SAND

J.E. Crum

AHMAD, YOU WON'T DIE A MEXICAN

Ahmad Tahriri

Why do they make the containers for ashes like a mini coffin? I remember walking with it and thinking that people watching might have thought a baby died. I think that's unfair to the onlookers. Why not make it like a bowling ball that I could roll across the field and into the shallow grave? Or a soccer ball?[1] Give me a chance to get cheers. I had no chance.

Before my mom died she wrote me a letter:

> *Ahmad, you won't die a Mexican. You never*
> *learned to roll your Rs. You should have died before me.*
> *Love,*
> *Your mom*

I didn't understand this letter, so I've decided to apply the following four-part investigation/examination that will hopefully lead to some satisfying conclusion or at least something conclusive.

I. HISTORY

I think I was doing a better job when I was in high school. At least by junior year I was working my way through a third year of Spanish, and I was dating a Mexican girl (full on *Her Parents Didn't Like Me And It Took A Year For Me To Visit Their House* Mexican[2]). I had a black hoodie with a homemade EZLN patch,[3] I had seen "Y Tu Mamá También," I started eating the grey stuff floating around my bowl of menudo, and I had seen *Grease* a million time.[4] But like the Aztec Empire, all good things come to an end.

I wonder if there is a determinist historical perspective that can pair my high school years with some specific Ante-demexicaification phase. I think it would trace the following trajectory of an evolving cultural identity:

1. Blank/Appeal to broad sensory stimulation (toddler)
2. An appeal to the generic (childhood)
3. A rejection of the generic (adolescence)
4. An embrace of heritage (teenage/elderly [5])

I must have been at the last phase, and therefore the fall was inevitable.

Maybe some Braudelian/Annalesian historian could consider the growing cost of El Millagro Corn Tortillas[6] in the South Suburbs of Chicago and its effect on carbohydrate meal seeking and subsequent shifts in cultural appropriation. I can't recall now—but what if one day I walked into Country Squire looking for El Millagro, then noticing the price hike, walked mindlessly toward the focaccia, the pita, or worst yet . . . the bagel. There's possibly some macro data that resolve all attempts at cultural appropriation and the corresponding conflict arising as a result. When a Caucasian Cubano Gastropub opens in Chicago maybe it's simply because the cost of angus from Northern Wisconsin has gone too high, so the would-be burger barn was scrapped for a pork sandwich.

I'm not comfortable with this for a personal explanation, but it does seem to follow this line of a lot of little big things slowly massaging your identity into something else. I think that makes sense to me. Though, I just can't remember enough. History is this odd thing, where you're trying to recount and reconstruct while only being able to hold so many pieces of information together at once. It almost demands that you look for the big moments that everyone can point to as the thing that everything else is reacting to. It's about finding the moment that can exist as part of a collective memory to give a template for each subjective story.

Since I started with high school, can I say the moment was leaving high school? Does it seem too simple to say that everything changes when you leave high school? Can I say it was being dumped by my girlfriend? Or is that too simple, too?[7]

It's too much for me to sort through. I'll just blame the tortillas.

II. SCIENCE

If there is one thing we can all agree it's that casual attempts to weaponize science for creativity is disgusting. Scientists spend a lifetime attempting to understand and challenge scientific concepts, so for a poet to casually browse a Wikipedia page or read a Brian Greene book[8] and write about how quantum mechanics explains the random failures of their life is absurd.

However, I'm not being creative. I'm an investigator. I'm trying to figure something out.

When I reach for some science memory my immediate thought is sitting in the front row of my first-grade classroom. The teacher was talking about something . . . and I was holding my pencil in my hand. Back then our pencils were always very sharp because the only break from sitting in class was getting up to sharpen your pencil[9]. I remember holding the pencil with the sharp end pulled back toward me like a catapult, and without thinking I flung it forward at my teacher. It nearly hit her in the face and she looked back at me with more anger than I had ever seen in any adult.

I wonder what the Iberian Beakers would have used the word casta for before Borja? Would they look into Mestizoic eyes and search for the next placement after chordata? Is there something special there? How does environment affect Mestizo genetic expression, specifically in the context of Schlichting and Pigliucci's (1993) identification of plasticity genes as existing in the form of regulatory genes. Can you lose that special expression?

Explanation 1:

Rutter and Moore (2001) found that maternal care sped mass development and carrion consumption in the nicrophorus pustulatus treatment group during the initial post-hatching stage. Nevertheless, that same group experienced delayed progress through subsequent development stages, producing a zero-net effect against the no care treatment group, implying a parental influence during the later growth stages. Applying this result to Patient AT, we might contemplate that the postpartum development phase, while twenty-five years removed, would be impacted by 17,000 hours removed from maternal care.

Explanation 2:

Shamim's et al. (2002) paper "Differences in Idiopathic Inflammatory Myopathy Phenotypes and Genotypes Between Mesoamerican Mestizos and North American Caucasians" presents two relevant concepts:

> 1. White People and Mexicans are different particularly in instances of dermatomyositis
>
> 2. Mesoamerican populations' location near the equator result in the highest levels of natural ultraviolet radiation producing high proportions of DM and anti-Mi-2 autoantibodies

I'm from Chicago 2,882 miles from the equator,[10] and I don't have dermatomyositis.[11] It can then be extrapolated that as an environmental cause have altered my proportion of anti-Mi-2 autoantibodies. It has also left me unable to find any delight in pan dulce. The effect could also be degenerative to phenotypical expression, leading to a greater dulling of Mesoamerican genetic expression until I simply die an Ahmad.

III. PHILOSOPHY

I'm willing to accept this should be a footnote, but I have to start this section by saying I'm not excited about what philosophy has to offer. It almost feels too easy.[12] It's pulling apart the question into widening circles that you can think through in order of philosophical era.[13] Nevertheless, I'm not changing the investigative lens—I've already written 1, 2, and 4, so now I'm looking for an end in the middle.

I'm obsessed with this problem Žižek has with V for Vendetta:[14] what happens the night after? I think he said something like, "I would sell my mother into slavery to see what happens the day after the movie ends." Žižek uses art as a language for society, I think this moment is a problem for using art to speak about art. The problem is then, "how do we go further?" For me, it's, "how do we push abstraction to absurdity?" Let's return to the source: the letter.

DIALECTIC PREMISE 1: THE LETTER AS AN ILLUSORY CONTOUR

JIM: I have reviewed the letter from Sylvia and determined that it does not exist. The words, if they can be so called, have been crafted to create the illusion of something written, but nothing was actually written. If you shake your head from left to right quickly the illusion is disrupted and what remains is a blurry smudge.

GYM: Isn't blurry smudge redundant?

JIM: What remains is a cryptographic smudge.

GYM: If a previously identified letter is made to look like a smudge by shaking your head. Would that contradict your argument?

JIM: Yes.

GYM: *Shows a letter.* Is this a letter?

JIM: Hold on—let me check. *Shakes his head quickly.* No. It's not a letter. It's a smudge.

Conclusion: Letter might not exist.

IV. NAGUAL

Saler (1964), looking across several references in literature, found two categories of Nagual, broadly connecting the word to a shape shifter or companion. The shapeshifter is a helpful concept to maintain culturally. As an Aztec leader nodded to receive the Eucharist, I bet he felt himself sinking deeper into his own tradition as a Nagual. As a person faces the reality of their deteriorating identity, they must first think: maybe I'm a shapeshifter? Before seeing the threat to a cultural identity as environmental, it's essential to consider this possibility. If you've ever walked out of your house with the full confidence that today's the day you're going to talk to that crush at school, then you see them and instead dart in the opposite direction and begin looking down at your phone—then you might be a shapeshifter [reference not found].

The Nagual is something I learned on my own. It does not speak well as an explanation. There's something inherently dead about knowledge you did not inherit. It's why I cherish knowing that El Tunel was a movie theater before it became a dance hall, more than I cherish knowing that *Songs of Innocence and of Experience* by William Blake is more a meditation on the acquisition of knowledge than a lamentation of the youthful ideal.

When I walked out the back of my mom's apartment, I could see the lit sign for El Tunel. During the summer that back door would be propped open by a cinderblock as we walked between the back yard and the kitchen cooking outside. There was a corner store down the street from my mom's apartment, called the Michoacana. You could leave through the kitchen, run down the alley, and be at the store in two minutes.

I have to wonder if my mom ever watched me walk into the Michoacana, like I watched her dance through conversations with a single pas de chat (simple and deliberate). [I'm not sure if this is even a good analogy. I don't know anything about ballet, but there's comfort in obscurity]. Did she see my foot tap to the strum of a vihuela, like I saw her brace the splintered hand rail of her staircase to ease the pain of her sorrowful joints? As I get older, I feel the memories I have of my mom shifting from emotions to records, from a gift to a responsibility. They're a collection that I have the pleasure to die with.

> Dear Mom,
>
> *I remember I was born under Metztli and you remembered everything else, so now it's all gone. I understand your previous sentiment and appreciate the reality of it.*
> *Love,*
> *Your son*

It's bad to end a piece by referencing a dream, isn't it? I won't, but I almost will. The other night I had this dream I was driving in the car with some woman. [not my mom]. She said that she would be teaching a writing class that weekend, and she expected to see me and my mom there. I remember trying to get the words out, but I couldn't. The woman driving knew what I wanted to say, so she started to explain: You know there's a way to bring back people from the dead. Have you seen the Silver Night Owl? It's a picture of the devil—and then I woke up. I have no idea what that dream means.

Here's a question that no one asked me: What's it like when someone dies?

Answer: Have you ever had a problem in a dream? It doesn't matter what kind—just a problem. Dream problems aren't like real-life problems—they're persistent and spill across storylines (i.e. "Yes, I know I'm in a boat race, but I have to focus on my speech for the president").

Dream problems create a very remarkable sensation, a distinct feeling that is almost shocking to your entire body—with a dream problem, the moment you wake up, they just disappear. Nothing you can say will make that dream real for someone else, and if you spend too much time trying to explain it, everyone else will leave too.

---

1 A fútbol.

2 A google search of *Meeting Mexican Parents* will direct you to a yelp page on the subject. Advice from Cameron X is as follows: "Don't wear anything with a plunging neck line." My neck line doesn't plunge for anyone, Cameron X.

3 Sure the hoodie was H&M, but the patch was from an old Hanes shirt, so balance...

4 My mom loved that movie. Not sure if that's representative of all Mexicans, but I'm throwing it in the list.

5 I'll finish this list later.

6 El Millagro is the only corn tortilla worth eating, for legal reasons I won't disparage any other brand, but just embrace their supremacy.

7 If you agree with this point then you better keep that same energy with Salma Hayek and Edward Furlong, because neither are dating Mexican partners.

8 I do own The Elegant Universe and wrote a real bad play that has long since been deleted. Thank God.

9 It was likely something science related.

10 This was the first and only teacher that I had accidently called "mom." The worst moment in a student's life.

11 Chicago Heights, it's like Chicago only the tallest building is the hospital I was born in. My sister does, so I will likely disregard this explanation. Patient AT.

12 I'm not spending any more time trying to make this complicated by fitting in modal logic. David

Foster Wallace is better than me in this respect—and only this respect.

13 Despite having majored in English Literature, Rilke is the only poet whose work I've memorized word for word.

14. Hated this movie. See, not helpful.

62 SHADOWS

Ora and Benny Segalis

AN OFFERING

Olivia Pridemore

My brother and I came upon a shrine in Okinawa
where miko still make kuchikamizake.
Here—sipping rice wines fermented in
the cheeks of virgins, is the closest I've ever come
to intimacy.

> *I want to cleanse myself*
> *with holy liquid, bind our*
> *futures with Shinto vows. Home never*
> *smelled like matured cherry blossoms or*
> *crisp oolong.*

Adorned with azusayumi and armed
with tamagushi, miko are taught to bend
from birth. They don't even notice
when their knees
scrape the ground.

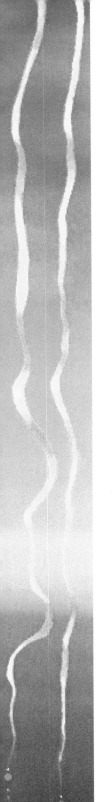

THE HEALTH OF MY STREAM
OR
THE MOST PATHETIC FALLACY

Thalia Field

Zhuangzi[1] said, "Let's go back to your original question, please.

You asked me *how* I know what fish enjoy—so you already knew that I knew it when you asked the question.

I know it by standing here beside the Hao."

1.

It was worth the perfect cliché of the land beside it (ruined old barn, surrounding vineyard, and olive trees beneath limestone cliffs . . .).

It was worth the extra line on the survey map (though I'm not sure it added any money-value.)

It was impenetrably, fundamentally, entangled.

Visibly obscured.

Fresh-water springs flow ceaselessly into it—from pipes, from catch-basins, and from village fountains that have slaked thirsts, saying: "Here's all the water you need!"

2.

Noting a chalked line on the bridge, a neighbor recounts an outsize storm in 1982 that washed out trees, vineyards, and the lower village.

A few valleys over, cliff-houses dropped from their perches into another panicked river. People died.

Consequently: "measures." Rocks beneath the bridge cemented down. The bed deepened. Fallen 'debris' swept.

3.

Only of faint concern during the life of the stone barn—not like the shivering horses warming the loft, moisture causing lime-scale to leech from the walls.

With the ruin transformed, hill shored up, muddy terrain planted, run-off redirected, town water and sewer permitted, certificate of occupancy granted—with all this accomplished, there could be meals and showers, and a toilet, and a dry bed for sleeping. Cicadas cool their daytime rioting, and for the first time I hear the river-voice rise like a question, close inside the head; closed mystery behind awake eyes.

Is it healthy? I never thought to ask.

4.

Without irrigation, the dry season brutalizes plants whose roots can't reach the groundwater stored beneath the clay.

But *owning* a few meters of bank, by right I can use what I can get—halfway out. A hose installed with pegs under the bridge, silt gumming up the pump.

Still, from this hose: lavender, trumpet vines, roses, star-jasmine, and wisteria. Apricot, cherry, and plums fruiting. Butterfly bushes and massive oleander, bay, viburnum, and borders of wildflowers and sage.

From this: hummingbird moths, a thousand butterflies, many kinds of bees, wasps, wood pigeons gliding from the high oaks to the lower ones. The occasional heron. The rarer hawk. Curious gangs of jays. Plunging yellow songbirds.

Fragments cared for, named, organized into busy sentences of ants and geckos and shaded scorpions, the sunning mantis, the long-horned beetle, the wolf-spider webs.

Twilight gnats and mosquitos, hunted by dragonflies, swallows, and finally bats; outlasting the remainder of church bells, the garrulous river rejoins a sky transfixed by stars.

5.

Foreign, awkward, I hear out a *vigneron* barely veiling his threats.

We walk the few hundred meters of vines, edged with the scrappy acacias, oaks, poplars, walnut, fig, bamboo, nettle— all thick and skeletal with bramble and ivy; more of the river's open secret than I had wanted to consider.

It takes three years to pay off those eight diagonal rows of vines, cash.

I didn't want the vines, with all the chemical sprays and ongoing minders and tenders. I bonfire the gnarled bodies. Turn the soil with paid equipment in the rainy season so it will one day get clean; the runoff will get clean.

Poppies, marigolds, sunflower, wild mustard, olives, almonds, loquats argue for the now-vacant field. Mice and snakes skirt the ant holes, hills, the wasp and bee nests; architectures of dessication. Foxes and boar cut across. Birds collect. Caterpillars hatch. Pollinators work. Feral cats make mischief.

6.

Invisibility nags.

Audibility teases. Always right before me, what I can't see. Fear infuses intuition.

Tease, tempt, taunt, dare? Sounds blind.

Have it all cleared.

Especially the nettle trees and bramble.

Save healthy poplar, oak, a few wild box, and one small expanse of blackberry, minding its gift to birds, and delicious August fruit.

Sunlight everywhere.

On the other slope, the one I don't own, can't touch, a walking path comes into view. Other people's lives.

7.

A stream looks smaller than it sounds. Narrower. I peer and mark it along my three hundred meters. And where my eyes go, so do sun-streaked turbulences and gravel runs, putting a face to jumps and falls. Here in plain view, the corpus shows its breath, its play, its dawdling, its means, its propositions.

Now I see dragonflies patrolling out of sight and zooming back. Water-hoppers stick the tension. Moss on balded rocks, shuttled leaves.

I had sensed it faintly, but now I locate a spring, crackling down the overgrowth on the opposing bank. A single hornet. Damselflies. A snake glides sideways, but when I check online, it's a lizard without legs.

Options for new projects appear, as though appended to the revealed scene.

I commission a "secret garden," just above the usual high-water mark, but below the level of the field. A quiet bench, a small table.

8.

A shadow turns and disappears.

In the deepest pool denuded of grass, where the flow slows and sunlight doesn't reach, just downstream of larger rocks churning out a waterfall: more shadows move.

Agitated eddies, and the reflecting light, protect them.

9.

Polarized glasses, and going out earlier, show me there are fish, caught in this sudden enraptured vigil. I am rich with time to spend; here to purchase their belonging, mine, I haunt the bench.

One fish lurks most of the day beneath an overhang. Smaller ones slip over a gravel rise between the deep pool and a smaller pool downstream. A darker, larger fish rushes the little ones as they enter the deep pool, scares them off, retreats. Several gather directly below the spring's trickle as though at an altar; rock near, circling.

It is July, August, scorching every day. A summer of persistent heat, no humidity, baked ground, brown but for the drought-tolerant greens in mid-sight: olives, cyprus, sage, rosemary, broom, oak, poplar, pine. Every day I sit with the fish, following their movements, the insects, the grasses, the skirting suddenness of the waterfall's repeating, the languid way lives persist in the relentless flow for hours and hours, I am moved; a becoming that feels more like myself than I've felt in a long time. In love with a life that has fish in it.

10.

A few days before I'm set to leave, a blast explodes from the crackling trickle, a rancid cloud blooming in the water, reeking of excrement. A bomb; fish surrounded, scatter, a chaos of dissolved paper, weird strings, plastic.

Too late, my phone can't catch it, the stench impossible anyway.

I start to cry. Foam the color of overcooked vegetables in the water, in danger, wherever that is. The fish are gone.

The tearful horror slowly un-clots downstream.

Night resolves; the fish are back the next morning. Joyful staring until dark by their side.

11.

A repeat explosion the next day.

I get waders and go in to look.

The crackling trickle falls from a broken pipe jutting from a gash in the slope, coating the cascade of rock in something slimy that stinks of over-rich waste.

Investigate: a new horse barn across the way. A shack used by local men to carve and cook up wild boar in hunting season. Road work done. Electric lines dug. Straight up the steep bank, a town water-pump lets farmers fill their tractor tanks. There is an open grate, would caravans empty their septics? Or pipes from the upper village? Centuries old, ignored.

I visit the town secretary, describing the problem without mentioning the fish.

(I'm not here most of the year; I fear that indicating there are fish, and someone will fish them. This is a rural place. Pilfering seems the rule. Truffles, wild asparagus, mushrooms, fruits, olives, nuts. Possession is only presence.)

The secretary says there is a woman with an old house not on the modern system. She'll look into it.

12.

I must leave and go back to work, in my own country—though my stream is all I hold in mind. My fish, their daily circuits, their daring forays, the way they stay still in such strong currents, in shadow, even their strange attraction to the pipe's trickle.

13.

The man who helps me with planting and large projects is the only local person I tell about the fish, mostly to give him a threatening look and a finger to warn his workers from thinking it might be clever to fish them out. And don't even walk in the stream. Or toss in cuttings, or make noise with equipment. Nods. Promises. Nobody will interfere.

"Les poissons ne sont plus là."

He writes that the fish are missing the day before I arrive. It's March; I haven't been there since September.

Rushing to the bench, decoding the colors swirled in the water, the tails of bent branches that look for all the world like fish shadows, I pass a whole day. Two. Despair. A third fitful night, sad waking of loss. Purposelessness.

Four days.

I retreat to my computer.

In all my time in their company (was I their company?) I hadn't thought to figure out who they were. I expand photos, try to remember.

I decide they are brown trout. The range makes sense. The kind of stream.

I read: they prefer to hide, come out to "lie" in a favorite spot, in riffles or downstream of fallen logs, where bugs and edible things float slowly. They can be territorial. Prefer a certain temperature for oxygenating water, so they can be energetic. Otherwise they wait where it's cool, deeper, shadier.

They love overhanging banks, safely out of bird's-eye-views. They share space if it's limited, or if some are younger. They dig reds for their babies in the shallow gravel transition between pool and riffle, in even flow. Sometimes they leap for insects. Change color with their emotions and backgrounds. They themselves polarize light, and focusing from each eye independently, they see every direction at once.

Most expertise seems to come from those who fish for sport, most keen to lure them out: "the wariest and wiliest opponent a river angler can face." I stare from the bench, reading the contours and rocks that might mean something to a fish.

On my last day there, a shadow—and another, and at twilight I see two medium-sized fish in the smaller pool. I take video and photos, overjoyed at my amazing stream, the living miracle, fish, and myself the luckiest person in the entire world.

14.

Two months later—mid-May. An unusual spring storm pushed thirty centimeters of rain across dry ground, driving fast tributaries, runoff, surging dirt and gravel through the narrow bed.

The smaller pool has filled in; the deep pool's outwash has grayed in silt. I worry, pacing, the fish evacuated, shadow-less, injured, or worse—they are not here—how could they be? Their small pool and favorite altar is gone.

An unchecked impulse gets me in waders, with shovel and rake. It's just one pool. It's just a little stream. Certainly I can help. Rake out gravel from around the small pool rock, like a child plays with sand at the beach, collaborating with the pushy water to dig it back out.

Scour the field for medium-sized rocks, drop them around the pool as a barrier. Watch the water detour around them. Hopeful.

15.

Back again in early June. A second unusually wet storm destroyed what I had dug, stole the added rocks, and left more gravel and silt than before. It's supposed to be the dry season now, but it's raining as I wait for a sight of a fish. I think I see a dark curl in the deep pool. But it's not there again.

The computer, I retreat to an entire galaxy of expert "hydrologists" and "stream managers"—

They say: A healthy stream holds many populations, good water quality, vegetation, balance, aquatic life, and riparian zones and floodplains. Rip rapped banks cause erosion downstream. Keeping the shores rich with native plants provides nesting and roosting places, and overhang, shade, root systems for stability. A healthy stream has tangled roots and tree limbs in it, all the messiness that life and death churn out. Cleaning the stream takes away critical habitat for insects, fish, birds, amphibians. Channels should meander, flow apart, rejoin with abundant pools, undercut banks, boulders and fallen trees. Engineering a stream to flow in a straight uniform channel is to degrade it. Landowners are part of the stream's life, up and down, affecting each other.

To maintain a healthy stream, they say you have to understand the entire watershed, the overland flow, the groundwater table, the rainfall patterns. Watershed also determines the quality of life for fish, for example, who don't simply exist in one isolated stretch. Streams must provide cool spots and abundant dissolved oxygen so fish can breathe. This comes through logs and rocks that mix air and water in the flow, and lots of riffle areas. Logs and rocks from big to little provide habitat for insects.

Most importantly, the stream's course constantly changes as channels shift in storms, and runs and riffles move according to the flow and power of the current. A healthy stream changes with the seasons, but must always have a width-to-depth ratio of less than 10:1. A healthy stream has microorganisms, habitat diversity, deep narrow channels, and trout and mayflies and other species not tolerant of pollution. Pollution indicators: bullheads and carp, chub and minnows.

Floods need to spread out, riparian zones and floodplains to absorb the water energy so steep or sparsely vegetated banks don't erode. Too steep banks also force water to propel energy downstream. Having engineers come in and straighten channels, or put boulders along to fortify them, ends up doing the opposite, ruining all the habitat in the process.

Pollution comes from rainwater (air pollution), storm-water runoff, local vineyards, farming, traffic. Places with infrequent rains have the worst oil and hydrocarbon runoff. Silt and clay clog the gravel where fish and insects breed. This silt-in-gravel problem is called "embeddedness."

Finally, streams move in predictable ways, their serpent-like energy carves out one side and then the other. Other patterns repeat: waterfall, pool, riffle, and run . . . it's how the flow must operate. Dropping rocks where there needed to be outflow, a riffle and then a run, is plain nonsense.

16.

Waders, rake, and shovel. Can I do this better now that I understand more about how a stream works?

Clearly the gravel dumped beyond the deep pool has made the channel too wide and shallow for fish to swim up. So first, I sling silt to the banks, swirling dirty clouds downstream with every shovel. Then I rake gravel into a center island, inventing channels on both sides that might—hopefully— deepen in the corralled flow. Since I read that fish like to 'lie' where there are current seams, I try to create one.

17.

From the house with my coffee, a commotion reveals a heron flapping awkwardly from my bench-ledge into the taller trees. I run, but the bird's impossible to find.

Does this predator mean the fish are back? Or just a heron also checking, hoping.

My hand-dug gravel island suddenly looks like a self-serve counter for the heron. It takes two days to shovel it away, towering piles on either bank. I have nowhere to make this stuff disappear.

Still, calloused, bleeding hands, and things sort of look as they were before. Which before? I don't know anymore.

18.

I finally arrive for the summer. Heat of July. Every grain of gravel lifted miraculously from the banks, and the wide shallow run has grown wider and shallower. No small pool at all. The deep pool, however, looks deeper, the rocks of the waterfall having shifted, augmenting plunging.

Day after day, no fish to watch.

I see shadows, but they are only catches of branches. I can't see the river clearly with the happy memories of last year caught in mind.

I visit the bench a bit less, linger less each time. Without the fish, I can't quite love it as much here. Their lives made sense of the whole place.

19.

I trudge back to the village secretary who tells me they did work on the old lady's sewer, and to come back if I sense another problem. There are moments when the flow from the pipe grows stronger, but to my knowledge the stench doesn't return. No more paper or plastic. Problem, and fish, gone.

This year's humidity is weirdly high; moist southern air pushing, cold air bearing down. Violent, early thunderstorms explode in August, forty centimeters of rain in a few hours, boulders crashing downstream, water touches the bridge. When I emerge from the house and look around, I see large rocks tossed to entirely new places, including at the pipe-altar, making any future pool impossible.

Even the overhanging banks have filled in. Compulsively, I rake and shovel and pull some of that new gravel out . . . it drifts downstream, but the flow spreads too weak to re-carve the lip. If fish anywhere have survived, they will not come back to this spot. Bleak bottom of the deep pool is darker and deeper. A lonelier abyss. Put the tools away.

20.

A few weeks later, I ask my neighbor, tentatively, whether people ever fish in this stream. Well, they stock it down near the bigger town in spring, he says. But those trout never make it very far up. Certainly not up here.

But aren't there trout here? I ask.

No . . . there are chub, like there . . . to an eddy just past the bridge, he points. Some larger shadows circle. Are those my fish? We move closer to the railing and watch them for a while.

Those are chub, he repeats when I ask the name. They aren't susceptible to pollution, runoff, chemicals from the vineyards. This stream is not so healthy, he comments, though the more of us who buy up land and care to protect it, it may come back.

21.

I spend my few remaining days avoiding the bench, the river rushing strong with the added flood-water. A fresh smell of muddied earth, totally unusual for end of August. Once or twice, I think I see a shadow darting in the deepest part of the deep pool. I imagine there is a large fish still down where the storm's water didn't disturb her.

One stream-management article says to have a "stream vision" that you share with your family and neighbors. Given time, I read that streams can heal themselves.

To my neighbor I said, "I hope so," but hope feels helpless.

22.

What would it change if I said that when I arrived, one time, another time, I discovered that someone I loved had betrayed me to the core, over the span of many seasons? How might the story change to reflect that lives can shift in a terrible moment, even though from another angle, it's only the knowledge that has shifted? All the efforts one makes, how can they do anything if we can't understand the whole situation? Or how struggling to sleep through a single night can occur with any set of worrying thoughts about a future that is only itself a reflection of ignorance? How would it change any situation, the situation of the fish in the stream, the course of the stream, the whole watershed . . . seeing what isn't being seen alongside what is? The mind futilely revises as it tries to make laws out of water.[2]

23.

In at least one culture, rivers have been granted the right of personhood, in the recognition that they possess the imagination and sacred feeling of those who count on them.

IN THE HIGH COURT OF UTTARAKHAND AT NAINITAL Writ Petition (PIL) No.126 of 2014

Mohd. Salim . . . . . . Petitioner

Versus

State of Uttarakhand & others . . . Respondents

17. All the Hindus have deep Astha in rivers Ganga and Yamuna and they collectively connect with these rivers. Rivers Ganga and Yamuna are central to the existence of half of Indian population and their health and well-being. The rivers have provided both physical and spiritual sustenance to all of us from time immemorial. Rivers Ganga and Yamuna have spiritual and physical sustenance. They support and assist both the life and natural resources and health and well-being of the entire community. Rivers Ganga and Yamuna are breathing, living, and sustaining the communities from mountains to sea.

18. The constitution of Ganga Management Board is necessary for the purpose of irrigation, rural and urban water supply, hydro power generation, navigation, industries. There is utmost expediency to give legal status as a living person/legal entity to Rivers Ganga and Yamuna r/w Articles 48-A and 51A(g) of the Constitution of India.

19. Accordingly, while exercising the *parens patrie* jurisdiction, the Rivers Ganga and Yamuna, all their tributaries, streams, every natural water flowing with flow continuously or intermittently of these rivers, are declared as juristic/legal persons/living entities having the status of a legal person with all corresponding rights, duties, and liabilities of a living person

in order to preserve and conserve river Ganga and Yamuna. The Director NAMAMI Gange, the Chief Secretary of the State of Uttarakhand, and the Advocate General of the State of Uttarakhand, are hereby declared *persons in loco parentis* as the human face to protect, conserve and preserve Rivers Ganga and Yamuna and their tributaries. These Officers are bound to uphold the status of Rivers Ganges and Yamuna and also to promote the health and well-being of these rivers.

20. The Advocate General shall represent at all legal proceedings to protect the interest of Rivers Ganges and Yamuna.

21. The presence of the Secretary, Ministry of Water Resources, River Development & Ganga Rejuvenation is dispensed with.

22. Let a copy of this order be sent by the Registry to the Chief Secretary of the State of Uttarakhand forthwith.

---

1. Burton. *The Complete Works of Zhuangzi* (Translations from the Asian Classics). Columbia University Press.

2. Thirty-seven percent of native freshwater species are at risk of extinction. About the same proportion (thirty-six percent) of amphibians are at risk. For freshwater mussels, sixty-nine percent are threatened with extinction. Across the board, native aquatic species are in trouble. Overall, the extinction risk for aquatic species is significantly higher than for terrestrial species. For comparison, about fourteen percent of bird species are at risk of extinction.

GRATIS

Arabella Proffer

OBLIVION

Melissa Garcia Criscuolo

after Dali's *Anthropomorphic Cupboard with Drawers*

A female figure reclines,
tired, naked, and covered
by a bit of sunlight.
Her torso is a bureau:
six drawers, two knobs each for nipples,
a keyhole in the bottom drawer.
She harbors a man's possessions:
his gold cufflinks and silk neck ties,
his daily schedules, his fishnets.
His most secret affairs go in the bottom drawer,
locked up in her deepest interior. One day,
she'll rummage through his drawers
in hopes of finding some semblance
of the man she knows intimately, perhaps
a note that smells of her jasmine perfume—instead,
she'll find small bird bones, a snail shell,
a tiny, spinning spider.

YEARNING

Öznur Kutkan

Translated By Vuslat D. Katsanis

Mesmerizing scents came to her nose, though she didn't know from where. She was turning her head right and left. As if trying to absorb the smell, she was lifting her head, wanting to come closer to it. This pleasant smell, which she couldn't quite place, was like the scent of walnut leaves, chestnut, and linden. Suddenly, she saw her mother's hair. Those dark brown, glossy tresses lightly touched her nose then disappeared. The smell suddenly disappeared. She could no longer feel it . . . .

The girl gently straightened from where she was. She realized she was sitting in her bed. A thin ten-year-old, she was an introverted, sad child. Am I dreaming again, she wondered. Where was the smell that came to her nose every night; the waves of hair that she felt on her face, her mother's thick, linden-scented hair, dyed in walnut leaves and chestnut?

She lowered her feet off the bed, wore her slippers, and stood up. She yearned to find the smell . . . . Walking slowly and timidly, she left the room, passed the corridor, and pushed the door half open. In the garden was a rather large well. It was very strange. Even though they had lived in this pink mansion for all those years, she didn't remember ever seeing this well before. The fear inside her turned into curiosity, and with careful steps, she reached the well. She knelt down and looked inside. Deep below, ripples of water were first expanding then dissolving, then lightly forming waves again right through the middle, as if little pebbles were being tossed into it. That smell was coming from here. Brown chestnuts,

linden, walnut leaves; the water was rippling like her mother's thick, wavy hair.

This had to be a wishing well.

If I could just find a rock and throw it in, my mother would come; the thought excited her. She looked around and began searching. She searched everywhere but could not find even a single pebble in that grassy-green, flower-covered garden. Thinking, I must find something inside, she started heading toward the house. While searching the corridor, she noticed the hideous mud colored cloth hanging from the wall down to the floor. She didn't like that cloth. It was such a tasteless thing. She dragged it down on the ground. Behind it was a gigantic mirror. A girl stared back at her through its engraved, glittered frame. She looked so much like her with those large eyes and messy tresses. Deep blue or green, perhaps even grey, cold stares that she couldn't quite decipher. Was she frightened? No, she just wasn't able to make any sense. Even her pajamas were identical to hers . . . . She took a few steps back, looked at the girl's feet. She had on pointed satin slippers, just like hers.

Suddenly, she remembered the wishing well. She was going to find something to throw into the well and wish for her mother's return, while the linden-scented water, tinged with the color of chestnut and walnut leaves, continued to ripple . . . . Yet she couldn't find anything. She didn't even know what she was looking for.

Unaware that her steps were leading her to her room, she kept walking. She slowly took off her slippers and entered her bed . . . . The girl in the garden, the girl in the mirror, the girl laying in her bed . . . were they all the same girl? Where was that amazing smell tinged with scents of linden, chestnut and walnut leaves; her mother's thick, wavy hair? Was it in her bedroom all along or did it come from the well? She couldn't understand . . . . She couldn't know . . . . She felt tired. Lifting the duvet over her head, she closed her eyes. She had long fallen deep asleep . . . .

ÖZLEM

Öznur Kutkan

[Original Turkish]

Burnuna nereden geldiğini bilemediği mis gibi kokular geliyordu. Başını sağa sola çeviriyordu. Kokuyu içine çekmeye çalışır gibi, başını kaldırıyor, kokuya yaklaşmak istiyordu. Tarif edemediği bu hoş koku ceviz yaprakları, kestane, ıhlamur kokusuydu sanki. Annesinin saçlarını gördü birden. Burnuna hafifçe dokunan sonra uzaklaşan o dalgalı koyu kahve parlak saçlar. Koku birden uzaklaştı, artık hissedemiyordu . . . .

Kız yerinden hafifçe doğruldu. Yatağında oturduğunun farkına vardı. On yaşında zayıf, içine kapanık, hüzünlü bir çocuktu. Yine mi rüya görüyorum diye düşündü. Her gece burnuna gelen o koku, yüzünde hissettiği annesinin dalgalı, gür ıhlamur kokulu, ceviz yaprakları ve kestanelere boyanmış saçları nereye gitmişti?

Ayaklarını yataktan sarkıttı, terliklerini giydi. Ayağa kalktı. Kokuyu bulmak istiyordu . . . . Yavaş ve ürkekçe yürümeye başladı. Odadan çıktı, koridoru geçti, kapıyı araladı. Bahçede büyükçe bir kuyu vardı. Çok garipti. Onca sene bu pembe köşkte yaşamalarına rağmen bu kuyuyu daha önce gördüğünü hatırlamıyordu. İçindeki korku meraka dönüştü, yavaş adımlarla kuyuya geldi. Eğilip içine baktı. Dipteki su, içine minik taşlar atılıyormuşçasına genişleyerek hareler çizerek dağılıyor, sonra tam ortadan yine hafif dalgalanmalar başlıyordu. O koku buradan geliyordu. Kahverengi kestaneler, ıhlamurlar, ceviz yaprakları, annesinin gür dalgalı saçları gibi hareleniyordu su . . . .

Bu bir dilek kuyusu olmalıydı.

İçine bir taş bulup atarsam annem gelecek diye heyecanlandı. Çevresine bakındı, taş aramaya başladı. Her köşeye baktı ama her yeri çimenle, rengarenk çiçeklerle bezeli bahçede minicik bir taş bulamadı. Evden bir şey bulmalıyım diye düşünerek adımlarını eve doğru atmaya başladı. Koridorda bulabileceği bir şeyler ararken duvarda yere kadar inen çamur renkli, kaba saba örtüyü gördü. Hoşuna gitmedi bu örtü. Öyle zevksiz bir şeydi ki. Çekip yere düşürdü. Kocaman bir ayna vardı arkasında. Oymalı, yaldızlı çerçevenin içinden kendisine bakan bir kız. Kocaman gözler ve dağınık saçlarıyla ne kadar da benziyordu ona. Derin mavi ya da yeşil belki de gri, çözemediği donuk bakışlar. Korkmuş muydu? Hayır sadece bir anlam veremiyordu. Pijaması bile kendininkiyle aynıydı . . . . Birkaç adım geriye attı. Kızın ayaklarına baktı. Kendisininkiyle aynı sivri uçlu saten terlikler vardı ayaklarında.

Dilek kuyusunu hatırladı birden. Bir şeyler bulup kuyuya atacak, ıhlamur kokulu, kestane ve ceviz yaprakları rengine bulanmış sular harelenirken annesinin gelmesini dileyecekti . . . . Bulamadı. Ne aradığını da bilmiyordu.

Adımlarının onu odasına götürdüğünü fark etmeden yürüyordu. Yavaşça terliklerini çıkardı. Yatağına girdi . . . . Bahçedeki kız, aynadaki kız, yatağında uzanmış kız . . . hep aynı kızlar mıydı? Ihlamur kokulu kestane ve ceviz yapraklarıyla bulanmış o mis gibi koku, annesinin dalgalı gür saçları neredeydi? Odasında mıydı hep yoksa kuyudan mı geliyordu? Anlayamadı . . . . Bilemedi . . . . Yorgun hissetti kendini. Yorganı başına çekip gözlerini kapadı. Çoktan derin bir uykuya dalmıştı . . . .

POPPY'S QUEEN

Fierce Sonia

HISTORY OF OREGON

Gabriel Vigh

I. geologic

how many lives have come and gone
since Mt. Mazama shuddered—
opened that hot udder and spilled
wet rock skyward?
the sound like a perfect bomb.

if humanity is a stain,
the Cordillera, the Cascades,
unsullied, immaculate,
have been known to wait.

II. native peoples

he needs evidence, man.
needs to trace himself backwards, farther
and farther, until a hand emerges from dirt
holding a goat's horn,
a salmon skin.

a distant drum notices the silence,
seasons to taste.

now hoof beats thunder,
real as hearts.

a war has come
whose stakes are the flowers
in the open field.

a new door opens—
the dark gets in.

we praise our creator,
open palm and sing,

but rain will not come
only men and more men.

III. europeans

sweat on the brow, but also the brow.
the immediacy of thistle,
breach of a narwhal.

Cabrillo shouts at a stiff rock,
gestures to Spain and the boys come running.
now they skim across the gyre
towing beeswax.

they want the earth smaller.
a country of pure grass—worthless,
but a rack of antlers . . .

they divvy Oregon, 50-50.
half to the Brits, half American.

the tongues of foxes keep lapping,
the nightjars dive beneath the moon.

remember—
you were nothing.
I gave you
a name.

IV. pioneers

we come with a new nation in our heads
carrying swords, obscene disease.

bringing babies, bringing Jesus
by horse and wagon.

now we have neighbors,
an open world.

you judge fur lust but understand–
there was no different horizon.

we came as you come
from nothing to something

and do not see your place
in it.

V. modernity

what pilgrims are we—
crossing a mad continent,

mesmerized by boom and bust.
from Salem to Salem, town after town

where we thought better. one long river
from us to them.

I'd have it stop—you'd go on,
send a miner down the hole for fun.

are there veins of gold ahead,
electric curtains?

to be here babbling
there was someone cruel–

familiar eyes trapped
in a photo somewhere.

let's love,
ignore how mad it is,

be joyous, callous,
disappear.

SKIP CODE

Silas Plum

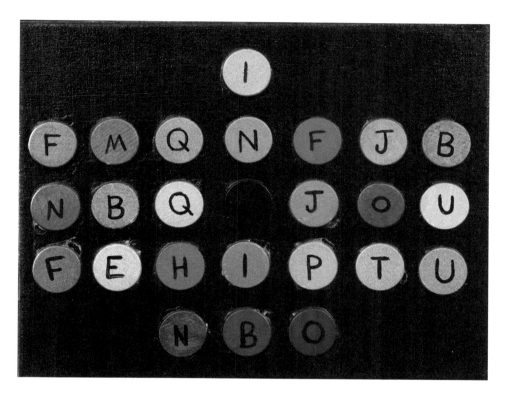

YANK

Elizabeth O'Connell-Thompson

Is it because I don't write about
wet stones stacked to mark a greening field,
the suck of mud trying to pull me feet first
back into the ground, or
the eye I plucked out of my own gorgeous head
and had set in a brooch to ward off all men like him?

I don't know how to convince you
that I am as much myself as I claim to be,
that I know as well as you do what it is
to return and find the windows shuttered against my gale.

My vowels will always be fewer, my tongue harder,
true as the grit from the wrong shore beneath my nails,
but I see this place for what it is:
　　　sand shifting before it's swallowed by the sea,
　　　no place to be buried.

HARDENING OFF

Elizabeth O'Connell-Thompson

After I scraped all of the honey
from the jar into my cup,
I brought it down to the garden pink with spring
and crammed it to the lidline with dirt:

Who knows when I'll be back?

Since then, I've made a life where the water
is saltless and blue and groans my name from under ice
when I get too near because it knows I am not its own.

Here—for now at least—
I am setting down baskets of fine, pale roots,

though at night I hear them creeping
toward that bit of home I stole.

DON'T TALK TO ME
ABOUT PROPHECY

Elizabeth O'Connell-Thompson

Everything I'm afraid of has already happened:
    the straw body staggering from the field
        to walk the ridgepole of my roof;
    the smoke in the shape of a man above me
        with my tongue twitching in his hand;
    the family quivering into a pile of snakes,
        ripping themselves open on holly branches.

I project them all onto the darkened kitchen window,
    review the footage as I pick penicillin from my bread
        and spread over it the red pulp of summer.

My ring sits in a bowl of milk I will leave outside tonight
    to poison with good, clean silver
        that which would steal the fat from my larder,
        the shadow from my step.

I am trying to explain to you that the clouds are the rain—
    they don't bring it with them.

CLOUDED CHASM II

Emma Arkell

ENSKIED

James Shea

A white
soft coffin
neither flat
nor deep
only long
and endless.
You live
side by side.

Day by day
a spotless
bliss, not
a speck
except
the sun
without
its shine.

RECOVERY TIME

James Shea

A pool of trees in a meadow:

devoicing me.

A book as a sort of passageway,

a way of passages to sort out thoughts,

passages that point a way out.

I'm a swimmer in the hills,

miles away from any pool or pond.

Foothills as footnotes to the sky.

Nature never slides back into place.

SOMA: BLOODY MOUTH

Yunkyo Moon Kim

You immure me.

Mouth is holding an ocean of blood. Seething with jealousy, I tuck the tropical fishes and tinfoil seaweeds safely into cheek to taste saltwater without casualty.

I am swollen with wisdom, though I am a celibate.

I am told that I am. Venus nurtured from foam and molar from a man's apparatus ascended to dismal immortality—I am sulfuric drunk ceramic kind of wet gaze plucked out of a fever dream, appearing suddenly in a doorstep wearing a straightjacket woven out of floss.

The thirty-two women are square jawed, crocodile-tear reptilians, glowing from exhaustion & heat with sick drywall sealer lips and crowns yellowed by cigarette butts. They're folding into skin and exhaling slowly under pressure.

Mouth is a purse holding its enemy close.

I wonder if I am truly insipid—if my hibernation is a phase desired by men who will then want to love me. My pinkness is a phenotype that offends Mouth, so I will wear red every month to confuse it. I always confuse perversion with romance, and replace it, like the aortic hip brace I shed last spring.

She asks me, sometimes, as if I had been fortuned to have become so famous overnight. Corporal immortal galvanized from the vulgarian Mouth wrestled from youth, as if to dispel it with mouthwash and stomach acid, I drain the Red Sea into the sink.

AUTHOR BIOGRAPHIES

April Alvarez earned her MFA in 2015 at the Sewanee School of Letters, where she is now the Associate Director. She lives in Sewanee, a town on the Cumberland Plateau of Tennessee, with her husband and two children. This is her first published short story.

Dean Barker has had plays produced on the London Fringe and Off-West End.

Marvin Bell's most recent book is *After the Fact: Scripts & Postscripts*, a back-and-forth with Christopher Merrill. His *Collected Dead Man* poems is due in early 2020.

Mackenzie Bethune is an undergraduate student at Saginaw Valley State University, where she serves as the editor-in-chief of the literary journal, *Cardinal Sins*. This is her first publication.

Margot Kahn is the author of the biography *Horses That Buck* (University of Oklahoma Press) and co-editor of the *New York Times Book Review Editors' Choice* anthology *This Is the Place* (Seal Press). Her work has appeared in *Lenny Letter*, *The Rumpus*, *Tablet*, *River Teeth*, *Los Angeles Review*, *Crab Creek Review*, and elsewhere. She lives in Seattle.

Clayton Adam Clark lives in St. Louis, his hometown, where he works as a public health researcher and volunteers for *River Styx* magazine. His first poetry collection, *A Finitude of Skin*, won the Moon City Poetry Award and was published in November 2018 by Moon City Press. He earned an MFA in poetry at Ohio State University, and is currently studying clinical mental health counseling at University of Missouri-St. Louis.

Melissa Garcia Criscuolo received her MFA in poetry from the University of Florida. Her poems have been published with *Mezzo Cammin*, *The Razor*, *Bedfellows*, and *The Acentos Review*, among others. She teaches writing at Florida Atlantic University.

M. Allen Cunningham is the author of several books including the new novel *Perpetua's Kin*, for which he was awarded a 2018 Project Grant from the Regional Arts & Culture Council. His work has appeared in many publications, including *Tin House*, *Glimmer Train*, and *The Kenyon Review*, and he is the recipient of an Oregon Literary Fellowship, two Oregon Arts Commission Fellowships, and residencies at Yaddo. He recently joined the English Department at Portland State University to teach creative writing.

Tracy Daugherty is the author of four novels, six short story collections, two books of essays, and three literary biographies. His forthcoming books are *Leaving the Gay Place: Billy Lee Brammer and the Great Society* and *Dante and the Early Astronomer: Science, Adventure, and a Victorian Woman Who Opened the Heavens*.

Emily Marie Passos Duffy's poems and stories are published or forthcoming in *Iron Horse Literary Review*, *Punch Drunk Press*, *Cigar City Poetry Journal*, and elsewhere. She received her MFA in Creative Writing and Poetics from the Jack Kerouac School of Disembodied Poetics at Naropa University. She lives in Boulder, Colorado where she teaches writing and performs burlesque.

Thalia Field has published three collections with *New Directions Press*: *Point and Line*, *Incarnate: Story Material*, and *Bird Lovers, Backyard*. Her most recent novel, *Experimental Animals (A Reality Fiction)* continues her interest in animal–human aesthetics and violence. Other books include two collaborations with French author, Abigail Lang: *A Prank of Georges* (Essay Press) and the forthcoming *Leave to Remain* (Dalkey Archive).

Jeff Frawley's writing has appeared in or is forthcoming from *Crab Creek Review*, *Beloit Fiction Journal*, *Bridge Eight*, *Pif*, *Storm Cellar*, *Gravel* and elsewhere. After receiving an MFA from New Mexico State University, he served as a Fulbright scholar in Budapest, Hungary, performing research for a novel. He now lives in southern New Mexico.

Camellia Freeman is a former Oregonian who now lives and teaches in Seattle. Her essays have appeared in *Crazyhorse*, *Image*, *Indiana Review*, and elsewhere. Past honors include Image's Milton Postgraduate Fellowship, an Ohio Arts Council Individual Excellence Award, and an OAC residency in Provincetown.

Brian Gard splits his time between Portland and Manzanita. He is the senior partner of a corporate advertising and public relations firm, which he founded forty years ago. "#42" is from a book in final preparation, *The Fifteenth Line*, from which poems have been published in *Word & Hand 1 & 2*, *Open Spaces*, *North Coast Squid* and *The Oregonian*.

Amalia Gladhart's short fiction has appeared in *Saranac Review*, *The Fantasist*, *Stonecrop*, *Cordella Magazine*, *Bellingham Review*, and elsewhere. *Detours*, a sequence of prose poems, was published by *Burnside Review Press*. Recipient of an NEA Translation Fellowship, she is the translator of *Trafalgar* by Angélica Gorodischer, and of two novels by Alicia Yánez Cossío, *The Potbellied Virgin* and *Beyond the Islands*. She is Professor of Spanish at the University of Oregon.

Robin Gow's writing has recently been published in *Poetry*, *Glass Mountain*, *Furrow*, *carte blanche*, *FIVE:2:ONE*, and *Corbel Stone Press*. He is a graduate student at Adelphi University pursuing an MFA in Creative Writing. He is an out and proud bisexual transgender man passionate about LGBT issues.

Sean Hickey is a teacher of English and Creative Writing at a New Jersey high school. His work has appeared in *LIT* and *Whiskey Island*.

Sarah Janczak's poems have appeared in *Colorado Review*, *Fjords*, *Tupelo Quarterly*, and *Witness*. Sarah studied at Sarah Lawrence College. She is a recipient of the Stanley and Evelyn Lipkin Prize for Poetry and currently lives in Austin, TX.

Alyssa Jewell is an assistant editor for *New Issues Poetry and Prose* and coordinates the *Poets in Print Reading Series* for the Kalamazoo Book Arts Center. Her poetry has appeared or is forthcoming in *Best New Poets*, *Colorado Review*, *Hayden's Ferry Review*, *Lake Effect*, *North American Review*, *Quarterly West*, and *Sugar House Review*, among other publications. She lives and teaches in Grand Rapids, Michigan.

Vuslat D. Katsanis is a writer, scholar, and practicing artist working at the intersection of multiple expressive traditions. She is currently Assistant Professor of Writing and Literature at The Evergreen State College, where she teaches interdisciplinary courses in literary arts. Her writing has appeared in *Interstitial: A Journal of Modern Culture and Events*, *New Cinemas Journal of Contemporary Film*, *K1N: Journal of Literary Translation*, and *Necessary Fiction*.

Tianli Kilpatrick holds a Master's in creative nonfiction from Northern Michigan University and a Bachelor's in creative writing from Allegheny College. She is an Asian-American writer covering topics that range from adoption to jellyfish to trauma. Her work has appeared in *TIMBER*, *Iron Horse Literary Review*, *DIAGRAM*, *Sierra Nevada Review*, *Split Rock Review*, and others. When she's not writing, she's riding horses or boxing. She lives in Shrewsbury, Massachusetts.

Yunkyo Moon Kim is a poet and essayist based in Boston. She was named a 2017 Grubstreet Young Authors Writing Program

Fellow and recipient of the Boston Globe Foundation Writing Scholarship, among other honors.

Leah Kiureghian was born in Germany and raised in Arizona. She holds an MFA in Poetry from Brooklyn College. Her most recent work can be found in *SAND*, *American Chordata*, and *RHINO*.

Öznur Kutkan is a Turkish writer, born in Ankara in 1953, and a graduate of Ankara Industrial Arts, School of Higher Education. After teaching industrial arts for nearly a dozen years in Elazig, Konya, Turhal and Izmir, she relocated to the U.S.A. with her two daughters. She is currently retired in Izmir, Turkey, where she continues to write. Her most recent work, *The Night*, is available on *Bosphorus Review of Books*.

Matt Leibel's fiction has appeared in *Electric Literature, Carolina Quarterly*, *Redivider*, *DIAGRAM*, *Quarterly West*, *Barcelona Review*, and *Bengal Lights*. He works as a copywriter in San Francisco.

John Paul Martinez holds a BA in Linguistics from the University of Wisconsin—Madison. His poetry is forthcoming or has appeared in *wildness*, *Figure 1*, *Rogue Agent*, *Matador Review*, and elsewhere. He was selected as a finalist for the 2018 Black Warrior Review Poetry Contest and has been nominated for a Best of the Net award.

Brooke Matson is a poet, educator, and the 2016 recipient of the Artist Trust GAP award and Centrum residency. Her first book of poetry, *The Moons*, was published by *Blue Begonia Press* in 2012. Her poems have most recently appeared in *Potomac Review*, *Prairie Schooner*, and *Poetry Northwest*.

Ahmad Tahriri is a short story writer and playwright from Chicago Heights, a city in Cook County, Illinois. According to the 2010 census, the population was 30,276. The city has a total area of 10.21 square miles.

Lori Anderson Moseman is the author of six poetry collections; the most recent are *Y* (*The Operating System*, 2019), *Light Each Pause* (*Spuyten Duyvil*, 2017), *Flash Mob* (*Spuyten Duyvil*, 2016), and *All Steel* (*Flim Forum Press*, 2012). Her collaboration with book artist Karen Pava Randall, *Full Quiver*, is available from *Propolis Press*. *DARN*, a poety/photography collection is forthcoming from *Delete Press* in 2019. A former educator, she founded the press *Stockport Flats* in the wake of a flood along the Upper Delaware River.

Elizabeth O'Connell-Thompson lives in Chicago, where she runs the *Wasted Pages Writers' Workshop* and works for the *Poetry*

Foundation. She is the author of *Honorable Mention* (*dancing girl press*, 2017), and her work has been published in *Poetry Ireland Review*, *RHINO*, *Entropy*, and *The Best New British and Irish Poets 2017*, among others. In 2018, she was a resident at The Moth Retreat for Artists and Writers and the Sundress Academy for the Arts.

Stacey Park is currently finishing her MFA at California State University, Long Beach. Her work can be read in past issues of *r.kv.r.y.*, *Foothill*, *RipRap*, and *Sonder Midwest*. She is a Korean-Canadian writer and also holds an MA in English Literature from the University of Toronto.

Olivia Pridemore is a multi-dimensional artist and cofounder of Silver Needle Press. Her photography, poetry, and comics have appeared, or are forthcoming in *Permafrost*, *Broad River Review*, *Memoir Magazine*, *Utterance*, *Sand Hills*, *Five: 2: One*, *River River*, *Bridge*, *The Ocotillo Review*, *Pidgeonholes*, *Round Table*, *Ampersand*, and elsewhere. Olivia lives and writes in Pleasant View, TN, where she enjoys spending time outdoors with her two dogs.

Robin Reagler is the author of two poetry chapbooks: *Teeth & Teeth* (Headmistress Press, 2018), selected by Natalie Diaz for the *Charlotte Mew Prize*, and *Dear Red Airplane* (Seven Kitchens Press, 2018), which was chosen for the ReBound Series and has been re-issued with a foreword by Laura Mullen. Reagler's poems have appeared in *Ploughshares*, *American Letters & Commentary*, *Pleiades*, *VOLT*, *Iowa Review*, and *Colorado Review*. She serves as Executive Director of Writers in the Schools (WITS) in Houston, Texas.

Peter Schwartz is a writer who lives in Washington State. He received a PhD in political philosophy from Berkeley, taught at the University of Maryland and Washington University in St. Louis, worked as the politics editor for *Microsoft Encarta*, and founded an online legal news and research company called Knowledge Mosaic that LexisNexis purchased at the end of 2012. Schwartz has published articles and essays on politics, history, and philosophy in peer-reviewed journals, edited volumes, opinion magazines, and literary magazines.

Daryl Scroggins lives in Marfa, Texas, and has taught creative writing and literature at various universities in that state. His most recent book is *This Is Not the Way We Came In* (*Ravenna Press*), a collection of flash fiction and a flash novel.

James Shea is the author of two books of poetry, *The Lost Novel* and *Star in the Eye*. His poems have appeared in various literary magazines and anthologies, such as *The New Census: An Anthology of Contemporary American Poetry*. A former Fulbright Scholar in Hong Kong, he teaches in the Department of Humanities and Creative Writing at Hong Kong Baptist University.

Dorsía Smith Silva is a Full Professor of English at the University of Puerto Rico, Río Piedras and her poems have been published in *Aji Magazine*, *Gravel*, *Apple Valley Review*, *Bright Sleep Magazine*, *Foliate Oak Literary Magazine*, *The B'K*, *WINK*, *Poetry Quarterly*, *POUi: Cave Hill Journal of Creative Writing*, *Adanna*, *Rigorous*, *Shot Glass Journal*, *Tonguas*, and the book *Mothers and Daughters*.

WLS (Wendy Lee Spacek) is a poet living in Bloomington, Indiana. She teaches creative writing at Indiana University, where she is earning her MFA in poetry. Her chapbook, *Psychogynecology*, was published by *Monster House Press* in 2015. Since 2016, she has served as the poetry editor for *Monster House*. Her work has appeared or is forthcoming online and in print at *poets.org*, *deLuge Journal*, and *TL;DR Magazine*.

Rita Stevens lives in southwest Michigan, where she writes novels about a small newspaper, and short fiction. She is retired from teaching in the local schools and as a writer and editor for a community newspaper.

Zack Strait teaches at Shorter University. His work has recently appeared in *POETRY* and is forthcoming in *Copper Nickel*.

Beatrice Szymkowiak is French-American writer. She graduated with a MFA in Creative Writing from the Institute of American Indian Arts in 2017. She now teaches English at the University of Wisconsin-Milwaukee, where she is pursuing a PhD in Creative Writing. Her work has appeared in several poetry magazines, and her first chapbook *RED ZONE* was just released in Fall 2018.

Jasmine Throckmorton is a writer and equestrian, working on her family's farm in Colorado. She pursued an MA in Creative Writing from University College Cork, with the financial support of a Fulbright fellowship. Her work appears so far in *Quarryman*, *Soliloquies Anthology*, and *America*.

Gabriel Vigh is a thirty-five-year-old resident of Cambridge, Massachusetts. He grew up in a small town in the Ozark Mountains of northern Arkansas and has been writing poetry since middle school. In addition to writing he also enjoys composing electronic music and 35mm photography.

ARTIST BIOGRAPHIES

Emma Arkell is a Canadian-born, Taipei-based documentary filmmaker, photographer, and collage artist whose work explores social movements, sustainability, the meaning of inhabited space, and mental health. She is fascinated by analog technologies. Her collage work is hand-cut, and she primarily practices film photography.

J.E. Crum is an artist who creates intensely vivid works using the method of automatism. Crum works intuitively to create art, finding inspiration from a variety of topics such as mythology. The artist considers art-making to be a journey of self-discovery as she creates personal narratives related to theories about fate, destiny and meaning of dreams of the subconscious. The artist also enjoys a career as an elementary art teacher.

Writer and artist Jeri Griffith lives and works in Brattleboro, Vermont, after stints in Boston and Austin, Texas, but her childhood was spent in Wisconsin. These disparate places each feel like separate countries to her, with landscapes, seasons, and ways of being that influence both her art and her identity. Jeri has published stories and essays in literary quarterlies and is currently working on a memoir and a collection of short stories, as well as organizing exhibitions of her art.

Fierce Sonia is a mixed media artist. She builds layers with acrylic paint and collage to create feminist funky futuristic fairy tales. She has a public studio at Torpedo Factory.

Through assemblages of defunct currency, discarded photographs, and long-forgotten illustrations, Silas Plum challenges the idea of objective versus subjective value. He believes strongly in the tired old maxim that the true value of an object is more than the sum of its parts, that the gut is a truth-teller, and that the Aristotelian notion of learning-by-doing is the best teacher around. Judge his worth at silasplum.com.

Arabella Proffer is a painter whose loose narrative themes revolve around a fascination with surrealism, medical humanities, evolution, and biomorphic organisms. She attended Art Center College of Design before receiving her BFA from California Institute of the